# The
# Doorway
## to PAM

# The

Doorway
to PAM

## Michelle Gordon

theamethystangel.com

First published in Great Britain in 2011 by Michelle Gordon
Second Edition published in Great Britain in 2014 by The Amethyst Angel
Third Edition Published in Great Britain in 2018 by The Amethyst Angel

Copyright © 2018 by The Amethyst Angel
Cover Artwork by madappledesigns copyright © madappledesigns

ISBN: 978-1-912257-31-7

Lyric from '*Waiting for a sign*' by Mary Beth Maziarz
www.marybethmusic.com

Third Edition

# Acknowledgements

First of all thank you to Mary Beth Maziarz for allowing me to use her music and herself in this book! Her music truly is beautiful and inspiring, and I would recommend a visit to her website: www.marybethmusic.com. Also, Mary Beth has written an awesome book called 'Kick-ass Creativity' which has kicked me up the ass creatively more than a few times while editing this book! So thank you Mary Beth :)
www.kickasscreativity.com

Thank you, Mum, for continuing to love me, believe in me and support me. I love you.

Thank you again to Liz Lockwood, for the editing expertise, please think about being my agent!

Thank you to my sister, Liz, for inspiring one of the characters and providing the setting for the scene, I hope to go there myself one day. Thank you also for designing the new covers for the Visionary Collection, they are so stunning!
www.madappledesigns.co.uk

Thank you to my two biggest fans, Annette Ecuyere and Helen Gordon, I hope you like this one too!

I also want to thank the following people, all for different reasons, but they will each know why! Emma Sanger, Dad, Mim, Dez, Meg, Helen, Chas, Cougs, Lulu, Jason, Charlotte, Ros, Lizzie Nicholl and Tom Dudziec.

Last, but not least, thank you, Jon, for your love and your faith in me.

This book is dedicated to my grandmother,
Evelyn Marion, for letting me use her name and for
making the best cherry and coconut cake ever.
(you can find her famous recipe at the end of the book)

# Chapter One

It was over.

She stared blindly at the dark road beyond the windscreen, unaware of anything but the pain shredding her heart into tiny pieces. Her grip on the steering wheel slackened and her shoulders slumped.

It was truly over.

After years of hoping, dreaming, wondering, wishing, fantasising – she had finally taken the leap and declared her true feelings.

They were not mutual, it seemed.

The sound of a horn brought her back to the present moment and she glanced at the speedometer. She was barely doing twenty miles per hour. She indicated left and pulled off at the first turning she came to, barely noticing the long line of headlights streaming past behind her.

Instead of coming to an immediate stop, she let the car roll forward at its own pace, until it finally ran out of steam. Her mind still clouded in pain, her eyes stinging from the tears that she refused to shed, she sat in the stalled car, the headlights still lighting the path ahead.

What really killed her was his certainty. He hadn't even wanted to meet up to see if they could possibly make a go of it. How could he be so sure? Did he hate her?

At this thought, a single tear escaped the confines of her red eyes and made its way down her ashen cheek. Soon, her vision blurred, it was as though the heavens had opened and cried down all the rain in its possession.

How could something that hadn't even existed in the first place hurt so much when it was gone? How could she have let her imagination run away with her for so many years? She was so sure that they were meant to be together. She would have bet her life savings on it - if she'd had any, that is. To think, she'd held back all this time from getting too involved with anyone else in the vain hope that she would one day be with him. How many amazing relationships had she missed out on? What if one of the men she had rejected was in fact her soulmate? She took a deep, shuddering breath and sniffled. What a mess.

She wiped her eyes with a tattered tissue then squinted and focused on the object she had been staring at for the last few minutes. It was a small square sign, lit up by the headlights of her car.

"Pam's Tearooms. Open 24/7."

She frowned. It was unusual to find a tearoom out here in the middle of nowhere, but one that was open twenty-four hours a day, seven days a week? That was just downright bizarre. She shrugged to herself and blew her nose. A strong, sweet cup of tea was exactly what she needed right now. Not to mention a trip to the bathroom. She reached over to the passenger seat and grabbed her handbag, then she switched off the headlights and got out of the car. Outside, the darkness was complete except for a small porch light above the tearoom door. The silence of the night surrounded her as she hurried across the clearing toward the welcoming light.

She hesitated at the doorway for a moment, then pushed the heavy wooden door open. The first thing she noticed was the soft music and the warm, cosy decoration. She relaxed instantly, it reminded her of her grandmother's kitchen. She glanced around and saw there was only one other customer there, an older lady in a blue knitted jumper. She blinked and looked again.

"Gran?" she whispered illogically, taking a few steps forward.

The woman looked up then and smiled. "Oh, hello there, dear." She got up slowly, her old limbs creaking and protesting. "I didn't hear you come in." She gestured to the counter, "Would you like something to eat? Or drink? You look like you could do with a nice cup of tea."

Overcome with irrational disappointment that the woman in front of her was not in fact her grandmother, all she could do was nod. The woman went over to the counter and got a teapot out. While she was filling it with hot water, she looked up and smiled.

"Why don't you join me, dear? I could do with some company for a bit. Oh, and the loos are through that way," she added, gesturing to the left of the counter.

Hiding her surprise that the old woman knew she needed the toilet, she went to the bathroom, feeling more comfortable and a little warmer when she returned to the table. She shrugged out of her jacket and sat down.

Within minutes, there was a steaming cup of tea and a huge slab of cherry and coconut cake in front of her. Unable to hide it this time, she looked up at the woman in surprise.

"How did you know that?"

"Know what, dear?"

"My grandmother used to make this cake, it was my

favourite."

The woman smiled and picked up her own cup of tea. "Just a good guess, I suppose. What's your name?"

"Natalie. Are you Pam?" she asked, referring to the sign outside.

The woman smiled. "Nice to meet you, Natalie. No, I'm not Pam, I'm Evelyn. Pam isn't a person, it's the essence of the place itself."

Natalie frowned. "Okay, well it's nice to meet you, Evelyn. I guess it's pretty slow tonight, huh?"

Evelyn looked around the empty room, a smile on her face. "It would seem so, yes. But anyway my dear, what brings you out here tonight?"

Natalie sighed and looked down at the plumes of steam rising from her cup. "It's nothing, really. I just needed to get away, so I thought I'd go for a drive."

"It must be important if it has upset you this much," Evelyn said softly. She reached over and patted Natalie's hand. "You can talk to me, dear."

Natalie was quiet for a moment, wondering where to begin. "I just feel so alone." She looked up at Evelyn and grimaced. "It feels like no one wants me, like I'm so completely unlovable. Everyone I have ever loved is either dead or has rejected me." She bit her lip, willing herself not to cry in front of a stranger. When a tear did manage to fall, she wiped it away quickly and tried to laugh.

"I'm sorry, I'm sure you don't want to hear any of this."

"On the contrary, my dear. That's what I am here for." Evelyn smiled and took a bite of her own giant piece of cake. After swallowing, she wiped the crumbs from her mouth and smiled. "Why don't you tell me the whole story, from the beginning? Perhaps I can help you to make sense of it all."

Natalie nodded. Usually she wouldn't dream of laying herself bare to a stranger, admitting all her weaknesses and discussing her losses, but there was something about Evelyn that compelled her to do so.

"When I was seven years old, my parents died in a plane crash, along with my grandfather. The only relative I had left was my grandmother. I went to live with her, in a tiny village called Waxford." Natalie smiled and took a sip of her tea. "Though I missed my parents, I adored my grandmother. She was the best. She played games with me, plaited my hair, and she gave the most amazing hugs ever. While living there, I met Phillip. He was the same age as me and lived next door. We were in the same class at school and we played together after school every day. I know I was really young, but I had the biggest crush on him." She let out a tired chuckle.

"I never said anything though, I suppose I assumed that my feelings were plainly obvious, and I was afraid that if I voiced them, it would change things between us. But I always assumed that he knew." She sighed. "When I was twelve, I came home one day to find my grandmother on the floor at the bottom of the stairs." She swallowed hard, struggling to keep her voice from shaking.

"She'd tripped, fallen and broken her neck. By the time I found her she was already cold. I had no one else left to take me in. Phillip's family tried to get custody of me, but for some reason they weren't able to. I was sent to a home that was over an hour away. I went to a different school and tried to make new friends. Phillip promised to come and see me often, but just two years later he met his first girlfriend, and he no longer had the time for me." Natalie paused to sip more of her tea, her pain evident in her shaking hands. Evelyn tutted sympathetically, but remained quiet, listening attentively.

"Despite the fact that we never saw each other, and the fact that he had a girlfriend, I never got over him. I still loved him. And somehow I still held the belief that one day we would be together. As far as I was concerned, we were soulmates – destined to be together, no matter what." She shook her head. "I've spent the last eleven years hoping that we would be together. I even dreamt most nights about him, about what it would be like to finally get to hold him, kiss him, be with him forever. Finally, I decided I'd waited long enough. It was time to tell him how I felt. He'd split up with his girlfriend, there was nothing keeping us apart except my fear of being rejected. I tried to come up with ways to tell him, and eventually settled on writing a letter." She looked up at Evelyn and smiled shyly. "I wish I could have done it face to face, but I was scared. Pathetic, huh?" Evelyn shook her head, a gentle smile on her creased face.

"I sent the letter, and waited. It seemed like an eternity before I got his reply." Unconsciously, Natalie had reached into her pocket and was now holding a very creased piece of note paper. She smoothed it out, running her thumb gently across the name signed at the bottom. After a moment, she handed the paper to Evelyn, who handled it like a wounded bird. As Evelyn read silently, Natalie closed her eyes and heard every word of the note as though she were reading it out loud.

*Dear Natalie,*

*Thank you for your letter. To say that it was a surprise would be an understatement. I had no idea that you felt that way, and though I miss our friendship, I'm afraid I just don't feel the same way about you. You were more like a sister to me, and I don't think I could see you as anything else. I don't think it would be a good idea to meet up, it would just be awkward. I'm glad to hear that you are well, and I'm sorry that I cannot return your feelings.*

*Phillip.'*

Evelyn finished reading and handed the note back. Natalie took it and stuffed it into her pocket without looking at it. Silence fell, broken only by the sound of tea being drunk, and the cups being set down.

"How is it possible, Evelyn, that another human being has the power to complete you," Natalie said quietly, "or to wreck you completely?"

Evelyn tilted her head and looked at Natalie thoughtfully. "You really have lost your way, haven't you, my dear?"

Natalie nodded, her features marred by the frown that was threatening to become permanent.

"Tell me, what did you come to this world to do?"

Natalie looked at Evelyn, confused by the question. "I don't understand what you mean."

"What's your mission in life? What are you good at? What have you always dreamed of becoming?"

Natalie sat back in her chair, slightly taken aback by the complete change of direction the conversation had taken. "Umm," she said, thinking hard. "I don't really know. There's never been a specific career that I've wanted to pursue. I hated school, I've hated every job I've ever had. I wouldn't say that I was particularly good at anything."

Evelyn's eyebrows rose. "Really? You can't think of anything that you are good at?"

Natalie shrugged. "I guess I'm pretty good at giving advice. When I lived in the home, the others would come to me and I would give them help and advice, even if I had no experience with their problem. I'm a good listener then, I suppose."

A smile had lit up Evelyn's face while Natalie was talking. Natalie looked at her curiously. "What?"

Evelyn shook her head, still smiling. "I never thought I would see the day," she murmured.

Thoroughly confused now, Natalie waited for her to elaborate.

"I've been waiting for you, my dear child. I didn't think you'd be quite this young, but it certainly makes sense." She clapped her hands together happily. "We have so much to do!" She stood and began to gather up the dirty crockery on the table. Natalie stood up and tried to help with the clearing.

"Wait, I don't understand what you mean. How could you have been waiting for me? I didn't even know I was going to be here tonight. I didn't even know that this place existed. Are you sure you have the right person?"

Evelyn took the dishes behind the counter and dumped them in the sink. She took the cup from Natalie's hand and added it to the pile. Then she rubbed her hands together.

"Where to begin?" she wondered.

"How about with an explanation of what on earth is going on here?" Natalie asked, becoming slightly irritated at being kept in the dark.

Evelyn noticed the tone, but her eyes continued to sparkle happily. "It will all become clear as we go along, my dear. Just relax and trust me." She was quiet for a moment, then she clicked her fingers, making Natalie jump slightly. "That's it. Yes, yes, that ought to be a good start." She reached out and took Natalie's hand. "Close your eyes."

Natalie frowned, but decided to trust her and closed her eyes. Seconds later, she reopened them and found herself behind the counter of what looked like a library.

"What the hell?" she exclaimed. She turned to Evelyn, who now wore a t-shirt that said "Pam's Bookstore" on it. "What happened?"

Evelyn smiled. "Welcome to Pam's Bookstore. We just had a slight change of location so I could show you what this is all about."

"A change of location?" Natalie asked, her eyes darting around the giant, book-filled room. "I don't understand. Where did the tearoom go? How could we be somewhere different in a matter of seconds? I think I need to sit down." She slumped heavily onto the chair behind her.

Evelyn peered at her, a concerned look on her face. "Hmm, perhaps this wasn't the best way to explain after all. Are you okay, dear? You look slightly green."

"Am I asleep? Am I dreaming? This can't be real, it's just, impossible." Natalie closed her eyes and rubbed them hard.

"Hmm, this is harder than I thought it would be," Evelyn said thoughtfully. She reached out and took Natalie's hand again. Natalie opened her eyes and blinked rapidly. They were no longer in the bookstore, but they weren't in the tearoom either. They were sat on a bench at the edge of a beautiful park. The sun was shining and distant sounds of children playing could be heard.

"What?" Natalie whispered, astounded. "Now I know I'm dreaming. I don't think I've ever had a dream this realistic before, but it must be a dream." She looked at Evelyn. "Please tell me what's happening?"

"Well, first of all," Evelyn reached out and pinched Natalie's arm, "you're not dreaming."

"Ouch." Natalie rubbed her arm.

"The reason that you found the tearooms is because you were lost. And I don't mean just in the physical sense, but in the spiritual sense. You feel like you don't belong anywhere, or to anyone. You feel isolated, lonely, like a lone ship adrift at sea." Evelyn looked at Natalie and smiled when she saw the girl nodding in agreement.

"It is only when a soul feels utterly lost, spent, alone, sad and full of darkness that they find the doorway to Pam."

"The tearoom? Or the bookstore?" Natalie asked, still very confused.

"Pam isn't just a tearoom, or a bookstore. Pam can be anything and can be found anywhere. It all depends on the person."

"You said that Pam wasn't a person, but the essence of the place itself. What did you mean by that?"

Evelyn nodded. "Pam is in fact an acronym for 'Purpose and Meaning'. This of course, is what every person in existence is looking for, even if they're not consciously aware of it."

"Purpose and Meaning. Pam." Natalie smiled, "I would never have guessed that."

"Well, we like to be subtle about these things, so that people can work it out for themselves. But you're different."

Natalie tilted her head. "How am I different?"

"Because you haven't come to me to find purpose and meaning, you've come to help me to help others find their purpose and meaning. This, of course, is your purpose."

"My purpose in life is to help others find their purpose in life?" Natalie mused, feeling the truth in the words.

"Yes, my dear. It is my purpose too, which is why I am here. And why I have been here for the last fifty years."

Natalie looked around the park, and her gaze came to rest on a bright blue butterfly that had settled itself on her left shoe. "Where is here, exactly? I mean, surely none of this is real? How can we be in a tearoom one minute, a bookstore the next and a park the next? I mean, even the time of day has changed." She gestured at the sky and the butterfly took flight, disappearing into the nearby hedge.

"It all depends on your definition of real, I suppose," Evelyn said. "You know you're not dreaming," she said, gesturing to the red mark on Natalie's arm. "So where do you think we are?"

"In my head?"

Evelyn chuckled. "That's certainly a possibility. But then, if we were, why wouldn't it be real?"

"Because I would be making it up?"

"So in your opinion, imagination isn't real."

"No, something is only real if you can touch it, hear it, see it, smell it or experience it," Natalie said. "If it's just in your mind, then it's not real."

Evelyn nodded. Then she reached out and picked a daffodil from a cluster of flowers to her side. She held it out to Natalie.

Natalie smiled and took it. She lifted it to her nose and inhaled its sweet scent.

"So by your own definition, that flower is real, is it not?"

Natalie stared down at the bright yellow petals. "Yes, it is, but I don't know how it could be." She shook her head. "I could just be imagining the feel of it, the scent of it."

"Is your imagination usually this realistic?"

"No, it's not. But I can't think of any other explanation."

"Have you considered that perhaps none of it is 'real'? That everything that exists is really just a figment of our imagination?" Evelyn waved her arm and the sky turned dark. The moon appeared in the sky and the sound of an owl could be heard in the distance.

Natalie's mouth dropped open and she stared at Evelyn. "Are you a witch or something? How did you do that?"

Evelyn smiled at being called a witch. "I didn't do

anything, it's all in your imagination, remember?"

"I never thought my imagination was this creative."

Evelyn chuckled. "We are all capable of so much more than we realise, my dear. The only limitations in our lives are self-imposed. Anything is possible." She let Natalie take this in for a moment, then she turned to look at her, her gaze serious. "All you have to do is believe that you can do anything, anything at all, and it is so. Now, the question is, do you want the job of helping others to realise this too?"

Natalie was quiet for a while. "That seems like an impossible task though. How on earth do I help everyone find their purpose? Help them to realise their own possibility?"

Evelyn shrugged. "The same way I do, my dear. You wait for them to come to you. You see, it's no good going out there and trying to help people who don't ask for it. They won't listen. Even if you can see they are struggling, even if you know what would help them, what would be best for them, they won't listen until they're ready. When they're ready, they will come and find you." She smiled. "Just like you came to find me."

"But I didn't come to find you, I wasn't trying to get to anywhere in particular, I was completely lost." She paused. "Physically and spiritually."

"Precisely. As I said before, it is only when you get to that point that you find Pam. 'The night is always darkest before dawn.'"

Though still quite confused about many things, much of what Evelyn was saying made complete sense. It felt... right. It was as if Natalie had known all of this before, and Evelyn was just reminding her. She decided to go along with it, and see what happened. She had nothing to lose, after all.

Evelyn seemed to read her face and smiled. "Are you ready now, dear?"

Natalie nodded and held out her hand. Evelyn took it and as the soft, wrinkled skin touched hers, Natalie closed her eyes.

# Chapter Two

They were stood behind the counter in the bookstore again. Evelyn glanced at her watch.

"He should be here any minute. Just watch me this time and see how I handle it, okay? Afterwards, I'll explain anything you don't understand."

Natalie nodded. She looked around for something to do. Evelyn handed her some books and a price list.

"If you could price these up for me that would be great." She winked at her.

Just then the front door opened, letting in a gust of wind and a few stray autumn leaves. A man dressed entirely in black entered, smoothing down his windblown hair nervously as he took in his surroundings. He went to the nearest shelf and started browsing, while Evelyn and Natalie busied themselves with the book pricing. Every now and then he would glance up at the two women. After ten minutes, Natalie was beginning to get impatient.

"What is he waiting for?" she muttered to Evelyn, while writing out a price sticker.

"Patience, my dear," Evelyn whispered back, her wrinkled hands deftly sorting through a box of books. "Don't you know that men find it difficult to ask for directions?"

Natalie had to bite her lip to stop herself from laughing, and quickly ducked down, hiding her silent chuckles.

"Hush now, I think he's going to come over in a second," Evelyn breathed, arranging her face into a neutral expression. Just as Natalie finally composed herself and came up from behind the counter, the man approached the desk. He was in his late forties, Natalie guessed. His dark hair was thinning and had a hint of grey, his face was gently lined. He looked up at them both and cleared his throat.

Evelyn looked up from her task. "Hello, sir, how can I help you?"

"Um, well," the man cleared his throat again. "I'm not sure if you can, I, um, need a book, I guess."

Evelyn smiled widely. "You've certainly come to the right place, sir." She gestured around the store. "We have almost every book in existence."

The man nodded, and looked around. "I don't know which book I need though," he said quietly. He shifted from one foot to the other and glanced at Natalie. She realised then that she had been openly staring at him. With a quick, embarrassed smile, she looked down and studiously continued her task of pricing books.

"It shouldn't be too much of a problem, I'm sure we can figure out exactly what book you need, sir. I'll just need to ask you a few questions to determine which section to take you to."

The man nodded, looking slightly apprehensive. Natalie listened carefully, her eyes still trained on the pricing stickers.

"Tell me, what is your name?"

The man relaxed a little at the easy question. "Clive. Clive Johnson."

Evelyn nodded seriously. "Okay, Clive, what's your

favourite colour?"

Clive frowned, and Natalie snuck a glance up at Evelyn to see if she was being serious. Apparently, she was.

"Um, well, orange, I guess."

"What's your favourite food?"

Clive thought for a moment. "Chilli."

"And what do you love doing more than anything?"

Clive's face lightened, and he almost managed to smile. "Being with my kids." The smile turned into a slight grimace and a tinge of pain entered his voice. "They've grown up now. I don't get to see them very much, but I loved being with them when they were younger. We'd go camping, fishing, or even just to the park to play catch." His gaze dropped to the floor.

Evelyn smiled gently. "I know just the book for you. Come on, I'll take you to the right section."

Clive nodded and followed her as she led him to the education section. Natalie tried her best to see the book she pulled off the shelf and handed to Clive, but they were too far away. Evelyn spoke to him softly and pointed to a big, comfortable armchair nearby. He nodded at her gratefully and settled himself into the chair. As Evelyn walked away, he opened up the book to the first page.

Evelyn re-joined Natalie at the counter and continued sorting through the books.

"I have no idea what just happened there," Natalie whispered, abandoning the pretence of pricing.

Evelyn smiled. "What didn't you understand?"

Natalie glanced at the man. "Can he hear us?"

"No, but we can go somewhere else to discuss this if you wish."

Natalie shrugged. "Here's fine." She set the books down on the counter. "How did you know which book he wanted just by asking four questions?"

"I didn't. The questions were just for his benefit. I knew which book he needed the second he walked through the door."

Natalie's eyes widened. "How?"

"I read his aura."

Now Natalie looked sceptical. "His aura? You're telling me you knew what he needed purely by the colour of the energy that surrounded him?"

"Yes, and no. The colour does give me some information, but most of the clues I get are from actually reading it. If you know how, reading an aura is like reading a book."

"Reading it? You mean the aura had words in it?"

"No, it has intentions in it. Thought forms. Ideas. Desires. Everything that a person consists of lies within their aura. It is a complete picture of them – which means of course, that it also holds the parts of them that they are either burying or haven't discovered yet."

Natalie looked over at Clive, who was reading intently. "So what book did you give him? What is his purpose?"

"Children. He is an incredible communicator. He knows how to relate to children on their level. The bond he had with his own children was so strong, it literally tore him apart when he and his wife divorced and she moved with them to another country." Evelyn tutted sympathetically. "He never really recovered. He's been wandering aimlessly ever since."

"When did this happen?" Natalie asked, curious.

"About five years ago."

"I don't understand. If he lost everything he loved five years ago, and was lost himself – how is it he has only come here now? Why has he waited so long?"

"That's a good question, and I'm glad you asked it."

Evelyn sighed. "It would be so much easier and the world would be so much lighter and more joyful if people came here at the first sign of trouble. They would find the answers they needed and they would get on with their lives. But it doesn't work that way. A person has to be at their lowest ebb, the furthest edge, the last straw, before they find their way here. Maybe they've lost the ones they love, maybe they've suffered a terrible illness, or maybe they've lost their job or got divorced."

"But that still doesn't make any sense. This guy lost everything *five years* ago, why has it taken so long for him to get here?"

"Because, though it was terrible, he was still able to carry on. He was still able to function. He thought that it wouldn't last, that there must be something better on the horizon. So he put his grief on hold and waited." Evelyn sighed. "But nothing better happened. Suddenly, five years had passed and he found himself in just as deep a hole as when they first left. It was at this point that he considered suicide."

Natalie's eyes widened and a small gasp left her lips. "Suicide?"

Evelyn nodded sadly. "He was driving to the nearest bridge, planning on jumping off it, when his car mysteriously ran out of gas and he found himself walking to the nearest gas station. Only before he got there, he found us."

"He was on his way to kill himself when he came in here?"

"Yes, he was. He could no longer see the point in being here. In existing. It was all just too much to deal with."

Natalie was quiet for a while, slowly digesting this information. The silence was broken only by the distant sound of pages turning.

"So you gave him a book about children?"

"I gave him a book that will help him to realise his own gift. To see that he is very much needed in this world. There are so many children who would benefit from his guidance."

"What book was it?"

"A book about Indigo Children. It's about the newest generation of children on this planet. They're very special, and I sense that he has just what it takes to work with them."

"How do you know that?"

"Because that is what he chose as his mission before he came to earth. We all choose, you know, on the Other Side. Our Guardian Angels help us."

Natalie blinked. "This is a hell of a lot of information to take in all at once."

Evelyn reached out and patted her shoulder. "I'm sorry, dear, I'm just so excited that you are finally here, I guess I am bombarding you a bit. Do you want to take a break? I can take you back to the park, or the tearoom. Or maybe you want to sleep for a while?"

"No, no. I'm not tired, or hungry. I'm just trying to process everything. To be honest, before meeting you tonight, I didn't believe in any of this. Life beyond death, alternate dimensions, life missions…" Natalie's voice trailed off. "I just figured that we were born, we do the best with what we have and then we die."

"That is the view that most people have. They have all forgotten what went before, which, of course, is the way it is supposed to be. If we remembered everything, how could we learn? Grow? Be challenged?"

"To be honest, I could have done without all the challenges," Natalie muttered.

Evelyn chuckled. "But without the challenges, you

wouldn't be here now, would you?"

"That's another question you have yet to answer. Where is here, exactly? Where are we?"

"Well," Evelyn began slowly. "Just now you mentioned alternate dimensions. This," she waved her arm in a wide circle. "Is just a layer of an alternate dimension that you are currently in. And before you ask if it is real, it's as real as anything you can imagine."

Natalie blinked, not entirely following the logic. "So we're no longer in the building that I parked my car outside of?"

Evelyn tilted her head thoughtfully. "We are, and we're not. Imagine the doorway to that building as a gateway to another dimension. The building that you parked" -she raised an eyebrow at the term- "outside of was your particular gateway. The building that Clive parked outside of, was his."

"So where, in the world, was the building that Clive found?"

"In a small town in Connecticut."

Natalie's eyes bugged out. "We're in America right now?"

Evelyn frowned. "No, not exactly. The gateway is in America, we're in another dimension."

Natalie sighed. "I'm afraid I'm just not getting this at all."

Evelyn patted her shoulder again. "You will, my dear. You will." She looked at her watch suddenly. "Hmm, another arrival. Do you want to see this one too? Or would you rather stay here? I don't want to overwhelm you."

Natalie stood. "I'll come with you, I want to understand more." She glanced over at Clive. "What about him? Are we just going to leave him here?"

"He's not going anywhere for a while. He'll be fine."

Evelyn held out her hand and Natalie took it, closing her eyes at the same time.

# Chapter Three

It took a few seconds to orientate herself when she opened her eyes. They were stood in the foyer of what looked like a hotel. A very expensive hotel, Natalie thought, as she noted the marble columns, the elegant furnishings and luxurious carpeting.

"They certainly don't spare any expense in this dimension," she muttered.

Evelyn chuckled and walked over to the concierge desk, her perfect high heels sinking into the deep pile of the dark red carpet. Natalie took in the change in her new friend's appearance and her eyes widened. Gone was the bright t-shirt with "Pam's Bookstore" on it, instead, Evelyn wore a smart light blue suit with a perfectly ironed, crisp white shirt underneath. She was also slightly slimmer and younger too.

"What happened to you?" Natalie asked, blushing slightly when she realised that her question sounded quite rude, almost accusing.

Evelyn laughed loudly this time, and it echoed around the cavernous room. "I have to look the part, my dear, otherwise it wouldn't be believable. You wouldn't see an old granny behind the desk at a posh hotel, would you?"

Natalie frowned and walked over to the desk to join the

now fabulous-looking Evelyn. "But you looked the same, aside from the clothes, in the book-" Her voice cut off as she walked past a giant, gilt-framed mirror and caught her reflection. She stopped suddenly and gasped. Slowly she crept toward the mirror, to take a closer look.

The woman in the mirror was stunning. She was dressed in a polished, pale lilac suit, with a contrasting shirt and matching heels. Her hair was perfectly coiffed in an elegant twist at the back of her head. Her make-up was immaculate. Natalie had never imagined that she could look so... professional. So poised.

*I bet Phillip wouldn't have rejected me if he could see me now.* The errant thought caught her by surprise and delivered a painful blow to her heart. She winced a little but couldn't stop herself from staring at her reflection.

"She'll be here in just a moment," Evelyn said, breaking into Natalie's thoughts.

Natalie looked up and nodded. She glanced at her reflection once more then joined Evelyn behind the desk. Blushing slightly, she looked up at the older woman.

"I'm sorry, I'm not usually so narcissistic, it's just," she looked down at herself. "I never thought I could possibly look this good. I know it's just a trick, none of this is actually real or anything, but well, it made me feel better, in a way."

Evelyn smiled. "The change may be an illusion, but it is not an impossibility. People can indeed drastically change their appearances." She gestured to her own, less wrinkled face. "Even look younger." She smiled. "And no, I don't mean by having plastic surgery. Ageing is something that is very much in the mind. If a person believes that by a certain age they will be old, then it will be so." She glanced at her watch again and shuffled some papers on the desk. "She will be arriving in about three seconds. We can continue this discussion later if you wish."

Natalie nodded eagerly and tried to busy herself with something, not wanting to appear too interested in the newcomer. She found a pen and a notebook and decided to start jotting down some notes on what she had learned from Evelyn so far. A small gust of cool air and a movement out of the corner of her eye alerted Natalie to the newest arrival. She snuck a glance up and saw a very well-dressed lady standing just inside the foyer looking slightly confused but perfectly at home in the luxurious surroundings. She hesitated only moments before approaching the desk.

"Good evening. Do you know of a good mechanic or garage nearby? My car just died, right outside."

"Yes, ma'am, of course, but I'm afraid he won't be in until morning. Would you like a room here tonight?"

The lady looked slightly annoyed but too tired to argue. "Yes please, if I could."

"Of course. We will have our in-house mechanic look at your car first thing and have it back on the road for you. Now then, would you like a garden or ocean view?"

The lady frowned, and even Natalie looked up, a little confused.

"Well, it's not like I'll be able to see anything right now, but I guess I'll take the ocean view, please."

"Would you like breakfast in the morning?" Evelyn asked, seemingly making notes on the computer.

"Yes, I suppose so. Is there any food available tonight? I haven't had any dinner."

"Of course, ma'am, that's not a problem at all. There's an excellent restaurant here, or of course you can call room service. May I just take your name please?"

"Yes, it's Dodwin. Janet Dodwin." The lady rummaged around in her bag for her purse. "Do you need my credit card?"

"That's not necessary, ma'am, we can sort that out when you leave." Evelyn handed the lady a giant key with a room number on it and gestured to the lifts.

"It's the first door on your left, second floor."

The lady nodded and walked toward the lifts. As soon as the lift appeared and the doors closed, Natalie turned to Evelyn.

"Okay, I understood nothing of what just went on, was I supposed to?"

Evelyn laughed softly and settled into the chair behind the counter. She gestured for Natalie to do the same. "Start with the first thing you don't understand."

"Okay, is her car really broken down? And do we really have a mechanic who's going to fix it?"

"No and no. Her car isn't broken. It was just the instrument the universe used in order to get her here."

"But why is she here? At a hotel? What answers can she find by renting a room? I mean, you didn't give her any advice or point her in the right direction or anything. How is this going to help?"

"Many people actually receive the answers they need most clearly in their dreams. In this dimension, their dreams are intensified and more focused. One night's sleep here could provide a person with a lifetime's worth of answers."

Natalie's eyes widened. "So what was her dilemma? What was her story?"

Evelyn sighed. "It's quite a sad one, I'll try to condense it down a little," She glanced at her watch. "We need to move on quite soon. Janet was married to a very successful businessman for twenty-five years. He was good looking, but quite arrogant and cold toward her at times. He never wanted children, and being a successful lawyer herself, happy in her career, it didn't bother her too much. Later on in their marriage though, she began to feel like she'd missed out, that maybe being a mother was something she would have liked to have experienced."

Natalie nodded again, she'd never really been bothered about having kids, but if she and Phillip had got together and he had wanted them, there was no doubt that she would have.

"I think their relationship had been strained for many years, so it wasn't a huge surprise when she found out that he was having an affair with a younger woman. They split up and divorced, and he moved in with his mistress."

"That sounds like quite a typical story. I'm sure there are millions of people out there in the same predicament. Why is she at her lowest point now?"

"She just heard through some mutual friends that her husband has not only married his new woman, but she just gave birth to twin girls and apparently he absolutely dotes on them."

"Oh," Natalie breathed. "What a bastard. That poor woman!"

Evelyn nodded sadly. "That's not all of it I'm afraid. It gets worse."

"Worse?"

"Her career is going through a rough patch at the moment, she hasn't got many clients and is having to work extremely hard to make ends meet. But the real kicker was this morning, when she found out that she was no longer able to have children."

"Jeez, it's a wonder that she didn't go and throw herself off a bridge like that last guy almost did."

"She's one tough lady, I must say," Evelyn said admiringly. "But even the tough ones need a little help sometimes. The main reason why I'm not pointing her in the right direction myself is that she's a very proud, independent woman. She would never take a stranger's advice. No, the answers she needs will have to come from her own subconscious to be of any use to her."

"So you really think that she will have a dream that will help her through this dark time?"

"I'm certain she will." Evelyn glanced at her watch again. "We have a few more minutes, do you want to see for yourself?"

"See what?"

Evelyn held out her hand. "Come with me, I'll show you."

Natalie reached out and grasped her hand.

\* \* \*

Before she could even blink, they were stood in a darkened room, the silence broken only by the sound of deep breathing. Natalie blinked a few more times as her eyes adjusted to the dark, and she realised they were in Janet's bedroom. She could see her sleeping form, curled up into a foetal position under the covers.

"Now then," Evelyn whispered. "I want you to focus on the wall behind her head, and know that you are able to see her dreams."

Natalie raised an eyebrow. "That's it? No magic words? I just imagine?"

"Yes, my dear. Now focus, we don't have much time."

"Okay," Natalie whispered. She turned to the wall above the head of the bed and, though she felt a bit silly, thought to herself: "I can see this woman's dreams."

Less than a second later, it was as if the wall had turned

into a giant TV screen. Natalie gasped in surprise and then bit her lip. She glanced down at the sleeping woman, but she hadn't moved. She looked back at the screen and watched, transfixed.

The first scene was a bit like an old black and white film. The bleak scene showed Janet wandering down a dark lane, alone. The grief was apparent in her posture and her face.

"Janet's had this dream repeatedly for months," Evelyn whispered. "She usually wakes up from it, crying."

"Is she going to wake up and find us here?" Natalie asked uneasily.

"No, because this time, the dream is going to change. Keep watching."

Natalie watched the screen intently, waiting for the change. But when it came, it still took her by surprise. Out of the gloom of the shadows, a man appeared. Janet, in her dream, came to a stop, unsure about this stranger. He held a hand out to her and hesitatingly, she took it. Suddenly it was like watching a film in high definition – the screen burst with colour and instantly the grief and despair vanished completely.

Hand in hand, they walked through different landscapes, illustrating, Natalie felt, that they would be doing a lot of travelling together. Finally, they ended up in what looked like a village in Africa. There, they helped out in an orphanage, and Janet spent her time caring for the many children there. It was easy to see from her face and her body language that she was incredibly happy.

Natalie wrenched her gaze away from the screen and looked down at Janet's sleeping face. Amazingly, the lines of worry had been erased and she looked lighter already. Her mouth was shaped in a content smile and her body was relaxed.

Natalie looked back at the screen just in time to see Janet kissing the man, as they stood at the altar. The scene faded then, and Natalie quickly wiped the tear from the corner of her eye.

"We need to go," Evelyn whispered. She grabbed Natalie's hand and the room disappeared.

# Chapter Four

The first thing Natalie noticed when she opened her eyes was the way the light was shining through the massive stained-glass window. It was so mesmerising that it took a moment for her to take in the rest of her surroundings.

They were stood in the centre aisle of a beautiful cathedral and the stone walls were lit up by the dancing coloured light coming through the detailed windows.

The second thing that Natalie noticed was that the cathedral was empty. The third and most shocking thing she noticed was that Evelyn was no longer with her. She turned and jumped when she came face to face with a kindly-looking priest.

"Oh! Father! You scared me for a moment there." She looked all around her. "I came here with a friend, have you seen her?"

"Natalie," the priest said, a hint of laughter in his voice. "It's me."

Natalie spun back to face him and her mouth dropped. "Evelyn?"

The priest nodded. "As I said before, my appearance changes, depending on what is needed."

Natalie looked down at herself and saw she was wearing

the same clothes that she had entered the dimension in. "Who am I supposed to be?"

Evelyn gestured to the pews. "You will be one of my only customers." She winked.

Natalie walked slowly to the pews, and sat three rows from the front. Evelyn made her way to the altar, robes swishing.

Natalie settled onto the pew and watched the priest (Evelyn, she corrected herself) perform rituals that had been practised for centuries. She was just about to whisper a question when she heard the creak of a door behind her. She glanced back and was surprised to see a young boy entering the church. He pulled off his baseball cap and sat in a pew close to the back. Natalie turned back to the front, not wanting to seem rude.

Evelyn took her cue from the boy's arrival and began the sermon.

"Welcome, my friends," she began, her deep, masculine voice carrying easily. "It seems to me, that there are less people now than ever before who still believe in organised religion." She gestured to the empty pews to emphasise her point. "And perhaps, this is a good thing. Perhaps it means that people are beginning to form their own individual religions or beliefs. Perhaps they are learning about all the different cultures out there and are choosing to accept and adopt the beliefs that make the most sense to them. And I applaud them for that. The world does not need more followers, but more leaders. More people willing to look deeper within and find their own way, thus shining so brightly, they encourage others to do the same." She looked around the beautiful cathedral, and her voice dropped just a little.

"But I wonder if they realise that there is still magic within a sacred space such as this. That there really is a higher power that wants nothing more than for us to succeed in life, to be happy. And that this higher power is listening. Always listening." She paused, a smile lighting her face.

"I know you are here because you believe that there is more to life than the mundane. I know you are here because you believe in miracles. So I wish to invite you now to join me in a prayer. Pray for something that your heart is longing for, that your soul is reaching for. Something that would make everything become clearer, that would make you feel like you have finally discovered your reason for being." She waved her hand. "Go on, close your eyes and pray with me now. I promise you that the magic of this place will grant your prayer."

Natalie closed her eyes, completely spellbound and believing absolutely in Evelyn's words. She thought for a moment. What would she pray for? She could pray for Phillip to change his mind, but for some reason that didn't feel so appealing anymore. No, she would pray to find the one who wanted her, totally and unconditionally. Who valued her and cherished her, who made her feel like no one had ever been loved as much as this. She took a deep breath and prayed silently.

"Please, God, help me find my true soulmate. Help me find the other half of my soul. Help me to find the one I wish to spend my life with, experiencing the ups and downs, and everything in between. Thank you." She opened her eyes and looked up. Evelyn caught her eye and winked again. It was so strange seeing her in a male body. Even more odd however, was how she was still recognisable, it was almost as though the image of the priest was merely a holographic layer laid over the top of Evelyn's form. Natalie blinked a few times, sure she could almost see the Evelyn she first met.

"Thank you for joining me for this special service. I wish you the very best, please do not hesitate to return should you need to," Evelyn said, a friendly smile creasing her face.

Natalie heard the creak behind her again, and she turned just in time to see the boy exiting the cathedral. She turned back to Evelyn.

"Will the prayers really come true? Is that what this dimension does?"

Evelyn made her way to Natalie and sat beside her on the pew. "This particular layer does do exactly that. I guess you could see me as a genie of sorts, granting wishes."

"What did that boy pray for? I have to admit, I was surprised that a young person would come to a church for answers, I was expecting someone much older."

"Yes, in the past the congregation used to be older, but there are some young people who understand religion on a different level. They see it as I do, not as a way to control people, but as a way to connect with the higher source. In years gone by, this church was full of people seeking answers on an almost daily basis. Now, I'm lucky to get one or two every now and then. People have lost their faith and trust in religion, and are now more likely to look for answers in a tearoom or a bookstore. Not that there's anything wrong with that," Evelyn added, smiling. "It just shows that times are changing, rapidly."

"My grandmother used to take me to church on Sundays, but I never understood it. All the talk of sin and sacrifice and pain and suffering – it didn't make sense to me. I didn't understand why people would willingly subject themselves to being told off on a weekly basis. But now, I think maybe it was the place itself that my grandmother was drawn to. Maybe she could feel the magic too." A tear escaped down

Natalie's cheek and she brushed it away, but not before Evelyn noticed it.

"You still miss her very much," she murmured. It was more of a statement than a question.

Natalie nodded. "She was amazing. She made me feel like I was the only person she wanted to spend time with. She made me feel like I was worth something." Natalie smiled at the memories that started to flood her mind. "She was always giggling. Sometimes, when something set the both of us off, we'd just be sat there, laughing until tears ran down our cheeks and we couldn't breathe." Natalie shook her head at the memory. "She was a fantastic baker too. Her cakes were without a doubt the best in the world." Natalie sighed. "There's nothing like waking up in the morning to the smell of freshly baked chocolate chip cookies."

Evelyn smiled and patted Natalie's hand. "I'm sure that wherever she is, she still loves you more than anything else in the world."

Natalie smiled back. "Yeah," she whispered.

Evelyn lifted the sleeve of her robes and checked her watch. "We have a while before the next one, do you want to see another part of the dimension? I don't generally have to watch over this particular layer, but I check in there from time to time."

"Sure, that sounds good." Natalie held out her hand. "Are you going to be a man in this next one too?"

"No," Evelyn chuckled. "Here, I can be myself."

# Chapter Five

Before Natalie could open her eyes, someone bumped into her from behind.

"Sorry!" she said, turning to steady the person. The young girl smiled.

"No, *I'm* sorry. I didn't see you there." She walked away and Natalie looked around her.

"A cinema?" she asked, surprised. It looked just like her local cinema: popcorn stand, junk food and a lot of people.

"It is the twenty-first century," Evelyn said as she moved to join the line of people waiting to pay for their tickets. "Moving pictures are now one of the major influences in a person's life. It's not really surprising to think that someone might find their meaning and purpose through watching a film, is it?"

"I guess not," Natalie responded absently. She was busy watching the people purchasing their tickets. "Evelyn," she whispered. "Where does all the money go? Is someone actually profiting from helping people find their purpose?"

"Why do you find that such an offensive idea?" Evelyn asked curiously. "Surely helping millions of people to find their purpose is something that should be rewarded in some way?"

Natalie frowned. "Well, when you put it that way, I guess there's nothing wrong with it. But that boy in the church found his purpose for free, why should these people have to pay for it?"

Evelyn smiled. "You're very observant, I like the way your mind works. And you are right, of course, if some get it for free then everyone should." She gestured to the ticket counter. "No one is really paying for anything. If cash is used, then when they leave this dimension it is restored to their wallet. If a card of some kind is used, then no payment is actually taken."

"Oh," Natalie said, feeling slightly foolish. She looked at Evelyn. "I hope you didn't think that I meant you shouldn't get paid for what you do, because that's not what I meant at all. Of course you should, you do an amazing job."

They had reached the front of the line. Evelyn smiled at the girl behind the counter. "Two tickets to see Natalie's Story, please."

The girl smiled back. "Hi, Evelyn! How's it going? Private viewing I assume?"

"Very well, thank you. Yes, a private viewing, please."

The girl tapped away at her keyboard for a second and two tickets came out of the printer. She handed them to Evelyn. "Screen seven. Enjoy your movie!"

Evelyn ushered Natalie through the cinema, and Natalie read the list of films as they passed by.

"Evelyn, how come I've heard of every one of these films except for the one you're taking me to see?"

Evelyn smiled. "Actually, you have already seen this film, you just might not have been paying very close attention."

They reached the door to screen seven where a young boy took their tickets, tore off a portion and handed them back what was left. The theatre was tiny, with less than five seats in front of a moderately sized screen.

"It's a good thing they're not trying to make money here," Natalie murmured as she sat down. Evelyn settled next to her, and almost instantly the curtains went back and the film began. It took mere seconds for Natalie to realise what they were watching.

"Natalie's Story. My story. This is a film about me, isn't it?" she whispered to Evelyn as she watched her mother on the screen cradling her as a newborn child.

"Yes," Evelyn replied. "Watching the story of your life is incredibly helpful in seeing patterns that you have been oblivious to. Which ultimately, helps you to figure out your purpose in this life."

"But I thought I knew what my purpose was now - to take over here for you? Isn't that why you're telling me all of this? So I know how to help people who come to this dimension?"

"Yes, that is your purpose, my child, for now. But it won't always be your purpose. I know it seems like each person has a singular purpose for being on planet earth, but in actual fact, each person has many – for different aspects of their lives."

"But now that I'm here, won't I be here forever?"

Evelyn turned away from the screen that was showing Natalie's first birthday and looked at Natalie. "Would you really want to be? Don't you think you'd like to re-join earth sometime, maybe find that true love you prayed for?"

Natalie's eyes widened. "You heard my prayer?"

"Yes, my dear. I heard it, and so did God. You have free will. If you wish to stay here forever, then you may, but I think that you, like me, will find that you cannot resist going back."

"You're going back to earth? When I take over here?"

"Yes, of course. You sound surprised, did you think I was dying or something?"

Natalie blushed and looked up at the screen, and saw herself learning to walk, much to the delight of her mother.

"Um, no, I just thought that you were retiring to, well, somewhere else, I suppose. Does that mean that you are from earth? A human?"

Evelyn laughed loudly, and it echoed around the room, briefly drowning out the voices on the screen singing happy birthday again.

"What did you think I was? An alien or something?"

Natalie blushed again, her cheeks now a very bright red. "No." She cleared her throat. "I thought maybe you were an angel," she admitted softly, embarrassed.

Evelyn chuckled again, quieter this time. "I'm afraid not, my dear. I'm just a normal, regular human being, like you."

"You're so good at helping people, though."

"I had a good teacher." Evelyn winked at her, then turned to concentrate on the screen. "I think this part is the part that really defined you as a person."

Natalie turned back to the screen and saw the scene that she had hoped she would never have to relive. It was the moment when the police had arrived at her grandmother's door to tell them that her parents and grandfather had died in the plane crash. She watched her grandmother collapse to the floor, crying, and she watched her seven year old self trying to soothe her while the policemen looked on sympathetically.

Natalie closed her eyes to block out the image but she couldn't stop the tears from falling or the pain from searing through her heart.

Evelyn reached out and gripped Natalie's hand.

"Even though you had lost your parents, even though your own despair must have been too much to bear, you were still trying to help others. You were still putting their needs before your own. You are a true helper and healer in this world. It is what you were born to do."

Natalie wiped the tears from her cheeks and opened her eyes. She turned to look at Evelyn. "Don't you think God could have come up with a less harsh way to help me find my purpose in life?"

Evelyn smiled sadly. "It was a harsh method, I will agree with you there. But there is good in everything. Perhaps if it weren't for that terrible time, you would have never have become so close to your grandmother. If you hadn't gone to live with your grandmother, you may never have found your way here."

"So you're saying that my parents and grandfather dying was a *good* thing?"

"No, my dear. But it seems it was a necessary thing."

Natalie sighed, and refocused on the screen. She saw time passing and her young self regaining some of her happiness. She saw her friendship with Phillip begin and blossom. Her heart constricted in pain again and she stared at the face of her very best friend and object of her affections.

She let her eyes become unfocused and tried to imagine how differently things would have been if her parents had still been alive. She tried to imagine how it would have been to have never met Phillip. She shuddered. As much as his rejection still stung, she was glad to have known him, glad to have had part of her childhood with him. She let her thoughts wander further, and tried to imagine herself with someone else. The idea that had seemed so foreign and wrong just hours – or was it days? – ago, now seemed interesting, exciting even. To meet someone, fall in love and get to know them as an adult would be quite something. As much as she hated to admit it, she could see what he meant about feeling more like siblings in some respect – he would always be the boy she swum in the local lake with, built fortresses with and grew up with. Perhaps a relationship would have only ruined those beautiful, innocent memories.

Natalie refocused her eyes and chuckled as she watched herself running around with Phillip, both of them caked in mud. As her life played out on the big screen, Natalie became aware of the patterns that Evelyn had mentioned. She could see how everything in her life had led her to this moment, and that everything that had happened was for a reason. Unable to help herself, Natalie found herself gripping Evelyn's hand when the scene where she found her grandmother came on the screen. She sniffed back another tear and watched her twelve year old self run screaming next door to raise the alarm.

Evelyn squeezed her hand reassuringly. "I'm sorry that I made you go through this again," she whispered. "But I'm afraid we must embrace everything in life, the good and the bad. We cannot have one without the other."

Natalie nodded, and bit her lip. Now the film was showing her saying goodbye to Phillip. She heard again the promises he'd made. To visit her, to write to her, to be her best friend... forever. They were such easy promises to make at the time, neither of them could imagine life without the other. But now, they just seemed like very easy promises to break.

"He meant it, you know," Evelyn whispered, as if in response to her thoughts. "But when you're that young, you have no idea that life will get in the way of promises like that."

"I miss him," Natalie whispered back. "Even if we were never supposed to have a relationship, I wish we were still close friends. I miss my best friend."

"It may seem difficult to believe, but I'm certain there will be other people in your life who you will love just as deeply, and who you will miss just as deeply when they are gone. The fact that you're not afraid to feel your emotions, and that you're not afraid to express them to others tells me that you are very much loved. And you too, will be very much missed when you leave earth."

"I don't know about that," Natalie replied. "It doesn't seem like I have any friends at all right now."

"Keep watching, there are many things you have done in your life so far that have reached people, that have changed their lives, and you haven't even realised. Every small act of kindness or generosity has far reaching consequences. Who knows who you might already have helped?" Evelyn stood.

"Where are you going? The film hasn't finished yet."

"I need to go and check on everyone, make sure they're okay. You keep watching, you need your concentration for the next part, anyway."

"Okay," Natalie agreed, a little confused. "Will you come back to get me when it's finished?"

"Of course, dear, I won't be too far away." With that, she disappeared. Natalie blinked and searched all around her, but her new friend was nowhere to be seen. She shrugged and concentrated once again on the screen. She was sure Evelyn would be true to her word and would come back for her. She watched the last ten years of her life, and began to appreciate what Evelyn was saying. She had already helped many people. Even small things like baking cakes for a sick neighbour, helping a friend out in the garden, giving her seat up on the bus to someone who needed it… all these seemingly insignificant things that she did on a daily basis without even thinking about them, added up. To some of those people, it meant a lot. It maybe even brightened up their day, or week.

She leaned forward a little when she realised that the film had reached the time when she had received the letter from Phillip. She clutched the letter in her pocket now, remembering the moment when she realised that all her dreaming had been for nothing. She saw herself, totally distraught, getting in the car and driving away from her tiny flat. It was irresponsible really, Natalie thought now. She should never have driven a car in the state she was in.

Once she watched her car pull into the lane, she stood up, figuring that this must be the end of the film. After all, she had ended up at Pam's immediately after that. But the film continued. To her shock and amazement she watched herself drive the car back down the lane to the main road and head home.

She sat back down with a thud, her eyes glued to the screen. Was it possible that she was watching the future? That she was watching what had yet to happen?

On the screen, Natalie's life continued as it had before, only with a few subtle differences. She was more confident, more sure of what she was doing, where she was going. She got over Phillip, and removed all traces of him from her life. She watched herself move to a new town and begin to socialise more, make new friends. But all of the faces except hers were blurry, indistinct. She made a mental note to ask Evelyn later why this was.

It seemed like no time at all before Natalie watched herself meet a man, and judging by the smitten look on her own face, she had fallen in love. She squinted at his face, trying to make out his features, but it was impossible. All she could tell was that he was dark-haired and taller than her by about six inches.

She watched in amazement as their relationship grew and they got married. Her eyes widened when she saw her growing belly and realised they were having a child. She took a deep breath then, and realised she had forgotten to breathe.

Time sped forward and she saw her family grow together, though her husband and little girl's faces were too blurred to see them properly.

"Like what you see?"

"Oh! Evelyn, you scared me!" Natalie wrenched her gaze from the screen and looked up at her friend. "I can't believe it, am I really going to get married and have a child? A little girl?"

Evelyn sat back down beside her. "Yes, my dear, you are." Then she waved her hand and the screen went blank, just before Natalie's daughter's seventh birthday.

"What happened? Why has the film stopped?" Natalie stood involuntarily, shocked by the sudden dark screen.

"Don't you think it's better to have some mysteries left in life?"

Natalie slumped back down into her seat. "Is that why their faces are blurry? To make it more mysterious?"

"There's no fun in knowing everything that's going to happen in the future. Besides, despite having just watched your future, remember it is just one of the possibilities. You still have free will. You may choose this future, you may choose another. It is entirely up to you and your actions."

Natalie was quiet for a moment, thinking over what she had just watched. "You said before that one day I might want to go back, rather than stay here forever. Is that why you showed me this? To make me want to go back?"

Evelyn shrugged. "Partially. But that's not the whole reason. You see, when we leave earth, and move onto the next world, we review our lives. What we did, what we didn't do, etcetera. It's called a Life Review. But of course, when you review your life then, it's too late to change anything. You can of course learn from your mistakes and try not to take them into your next life, but that's all." Evelyn gestured toward the screen. "By reviewing your life so far, you can change things now and not regret the things you didn't change or do when it's too late."

Faint noises could be heard from a neighbouring theatre as Natalie sat in silent contemplation. She sighed. Suddenly everything seemed so much more complicated, and yet her decision was to remain the same.

"I don't think I'm ready for that life yet. I want to stay here for a while, help people find their purpose, their meaning in life. Then maybe, like you, I will finally feel ready to go back and live my life with meaning. And purpose."

Evelyn smiled widely into the darkness. "My dear, I was hoping you would say just that. I'm glad that you want to stay a while, and I'm glad that you are going to return one day. I think you would make a wonderful mother."

"Thank you," Natalie responded quietly. She took a deep breath. "So, what's next?"

# Chapter Six

When they arrived in their next location, music filled Natalie's ears, sweet and longing. Natalie looked around the dimly lit bar until she located the source. A woman sat on a stool on the small stage, playing the guitar and pouring out her heart and soul through beautiful lyrics. Unable to help herself, Natalie closed her eyes and swayed slightly to the melody.

"She's good, isn't she?"

"Yes, she's amazing. Who is she?"

"Her name is Mary Beth Maziarz. She's been playing here for years."

Natalie looked at Evelyn in surprise. "You mean she lives here in this dimension too? Like you?"

"No, no, my dear. It's not quite like that. Here, come behind the bar and give me a hand, and I'll explain."

Natalie followed Evelyn and started polishing glasses while she waited for Evelyn to explain.

"Mary Beth isn't here in this dimension in the same sense that you and I are here, because she hasn't come through a gateway and then stayed. Rather, Mary Beth is still in the earthly dimension, but her soul visits here every night."

"Her soul separates from her body to come to this

dimension? So she can sing in this bar? But why?"

"Because she understands the importance of finding your meaning in life. She wants to help. So, while her body rests in bed at night, her soul comes here, in the hopes of helping people to find their way. Her beautiful music basically does my job for me. I don't really need to be here to help, but I just can't resist listening to her music for a while."

Natalie polished a glass thoughtfully for a minute. "Does anyone else do that too? Come here in their dreams, to help? Or is it just Mary Beth?"

Evelyn smiled as she cleaned the bar top. "Who do you think were the staff in the cinema? Who do you think keeps this whole dimension running? Dreamers. Souls who love to help others. They are all volunteers here. They might not remember in the morning where they have been while they were asleep but I'm sure a part of them knows that they are fulfilling part of their own purpose."

"Wow, I guess it never occurred to me that a person could fulfil their purpose while they were asleep. I've always thought of sleeping as being such a waste of time. It seems that perhaps that isn't the case." She looked back at Mary Beth, who had now put down her guitar and switched to the piano. Her voice was so soothing, the lyrics were beautiful. She glanced around the room again.

"Where is everyone then? They're missing the music."

"They won't be long now, there's quite a few coming tonight."

"Why do they have to come to this dimension to be affected by her music though? Surely she has CDs and does concerts and reaches people on earth anyway?"

"Yes, she does, you're right. But the people who end up here would quite possibly never normally come across her music, and also, being here makes them more receptive to the messages in the lyrics. Just watch, you'll see a few transformations here tonight."

Just then, Natalie heard footsteps on the wooden floor.

"Excuse me, are you open?"

"Of course we are, sir. Things are just getting started. What can I get you?"

The man looked around at the empty room then shrugged. He took off his jacket and settled onto a bar stool. "Can I get a pint of Guinness, please?"

"Certainly, sir, coming right up." As Evelyn got a glass and started pouring the pint, Natalie glanced at the man, and tried to place his accent. She hazarded a guess at him being Irish, but of course that didn't necessarily mean that he'd just entered the dimension from Ireland.

Evelyn pushed the pint across the bar to him, and he slid a note across to her. It was a five euro note, which answered Natalie's unspoken question. It still amazed her that people were entering Pam's from all different parts of the world.

Evelyn gave him his change and he took a sip. Nodding his head appreciatively, he looked like he was about to say something, but then his attention was caught by the change in song. He gazed at the stage, seemingly entranced by Mary Beth's singing. He picked up his pint, hopped off the stool and made his way to a table at the front, where he sat and listened attentively, only occasionally remembering to sip his drink.

Evelyn looked at Natalie and smiled. "I think he may have already found the answers he was looking for."

"That's amazing. Is finding your purpose in life really as simple as listening to the right piece of music? Or finding the right book? Or having a cup of tea with someone?"

"Of course it is! You don't honestly think that God made it difficult for us to find our purpose do you? *We* are the ones

~ 49 ~

who make it difficult. We make everything as complicated as possible, and then wonder why we end up floundering, lost and alone. Everything in life is simple. Easy. We just don't believe that."

"If we did believe that, would it become easier?"

"Yes, of course. You create your own life, just as everyone else does. I tell you what, once we've got the next two in and settled, I'll take you to a seminar that I think you might find very interesting."

"There's just two more to come?"

Evelyn's smile was a little sad. "Yes, the other two have just cancelled."

Natalie frowned. "Cancelled? What do you mean?"

"I'll explain later, the next one is about to arrive."

The second customer was a young woman, around Natalie's age, whose red-rimmed eyes and frown made her look considerably older.

"What can I get you, my dear?" Evelyn asked when she reached the bar.

"Just a soda, please," the girl replied, her voice husky. "I've never seen this place before, have you just opened?"

"No, we've been here for quite some time. Maybe you've just never noticed us before." Evelyn turned slightly and winked at Natalie. She poured the lemonade and handed it to the girl who suddenly looked ashamed.

"I just realised, I didn't bring my purse with me, I'm sorry." She pushed the drink back toward Evelyn and went to turn away.

"Wait," Evelyn said quickly. "Don't worry, you can have this one on the house. Please, stay. You'll enjoy the music."

The girl turned back and smiled uncertainly. "Are you sure?"

"Of course, my dear." Evelyn pushed the glass toward

her again and she took it.

"Thank you," she said shyly. Then she went over to a table, and settled into a chair. When the next song started, she looked up and stared at the stage, mesmerised. Her foot was tapping to the beat and her whole body relaxed.

"That didn't take too-"

"Excuse me!"

Natalie looked up in surprise, she hadn't heard the newcomer arrive.

"Could you possibly give me directions to the nearest town? I think I must have taken a wrong turn somewhere."

"Of course, sir, but how about a drink first?" Evelyn smiled sweetly at the suited businessman, melting his resolve to be in a hurry.

"Oh, well, sure, why not?" He sat on a bar stool. "I'll have a Martini, please."

"Coming right up." Evelyn winked at Natalie again and set about making his drink. Natalie found herself being caught up in the music again, this time by the lyrics:

"-and wondering if I, somehow wasted all this time, waiting for a sign…"

Somehow, it summed up how Natalie felt about the situation with Phillip exactly. She had wasted so much time waiting for him, waiting for some sign that he felt the same way about her. How much had she missed out on, while she was waiting?

The song was also clearly meaning a lot to their newest customer, as he took his drink, got up and moved closer to the stage, equally as spellbound as the other two.

"Right, that's it for here tonight," Evelyn said, putting her tea-towel down. "Let's get to that seminar I told you about."

Natalie nodded and held out her hand.

"Oh, hang on, we may as well open this up to everyone now." Evelyn clapped her hands and suddenly the room was full of people. There were even bar staff serving drinks, waitresses taking drinks to tables and bouncers on the doors.

"What the-? Where did they all come from?" Natalie sputtered.

"They're all dreamers too, drawn to the music. It's just easier to keep them out until the ones who need help have arrived and settled."

Natalie looked around, shaking her head in amazement. "I still can't believe that people come here in their dreams."

"Where else would they go?"

# Chapter Seven

"So, what kind of seminar is this?"

Natalie looked around the empty room in which she and Evelyn were sitting. There were several rows of chairs facing an armchair with a small table next to it.

"We're a bit early, but she should be along soon."

"Who is she?"

"Her name is Michelle Gordon. She does seminars pretty much every night. I think you'll find the topic of tonight's talk particularly helpful and interesting."

"Michelle Gordon? I don't think I've heard of her. Does she work here or is she a dreaming volunteer too?"

"I'm not surprised you haven't heard of her yet, she's not long started writing books and doing seminars here, but I'm sure in a few years' time she will become more well-known. When I'm not busy I love to sit and listen to her talks, she's very easy to listen to. She's a dreaming volunteer like Mary Beth."

"I'll have to keep an eye out for her books in the bookstore then."

"I would definitely recommend them. But I'm quite biased. I think she got a lot of her ideas from her experiences here at Pam's."

"Good evening, ladies!" a voice rang out, making Natalie jump out of her chair.

She looked up to the front of the room and saw a young woman sat in the armchair.

"I'm sorry, I didn't mean to scare you."

"It's alright, Michelle, she's new. I'm showing her the ropes."

"That's great. Though I hope that doesn't mean that we will be losing you, Evelyn?"

Evelyn smiled sadly. "I'm afraid it does, Michelle. It's time for me to move on. Live my life. I'm going to leave everything in the very capable hands of my gra- great new friend, Natalie."

Michelle got up from the chair and came over to Evelyn for a hug. "I'm going to miss you! You'd better come back and visit us here from time to time."

"You couldn't stop me if you tried, besides, I'll have to check in and make sure Natalie is okay."

Michelle released her and looked down at her fondly. "I wish you well, I should think the world is quite different now to when you left it."

"Yes, I'm quite looking forward to all the many changes to come, I must admit." She looked at Natalie and smiled. "As much as I have enjoyed my work here, there comes a time when you need to move on." She glanced at her watch. "Well, Michelle, you're up. Are you ready?"

"As ever! Let's get started." Michelle returned to her chair, and took a sip of water. About a minute later, people started entering the room and taking their seats.

"Are these people real or dreaming?"

"It's a mixture of both really, but mostly dreamers."

"Why aren't the real ones coming in first, like in the bar?"

Evelyn shrugged. "With the bar, it didn't matter when people arrived, they could still enjoy the music. With a seminar, it's more realistic if everyone turns up at the same time and hears the whole thing."

"Yes, I guess that does make sense."

It didn't take long for the room to fill, and Michelle cleared her throat to catch their attention.

"Welcome, ladies and gentlemen! I'm so very glad you could be here this evening. I see some newcomers here, I hope you enjoy it, and please, if you have any questions at all, please don't hesitate to ask them at the end."

She stood up. "I want you all, for just a moment, to imagine that you are not really sat in this room, but that you are in fact asleep in bed. Or that you are actually driving down the road. Or that you are wandering aimlessly through the woods. Can you imagine that?"

Natalie smiled. Pointing out the reality was an interesting thing to do, most of the people here had no idea they were in an alternate dimension.

"I want you to imagine that you are five years old. Can you picture it? Now imagine you are ninety years old." She looked around the room, most people had their eyes closed and were nodding. "Now I want you to imagine that all of those realities, whether they are present, past or future, all exist in this one moment right now. And that you are only experiencing this particular reality right now because it is what you chose to experience."

Natalie bit her lip. It was hard to believe that she had chosen all of the recent events of her life. It seemed too mad a concept to believe that she would choose to go through such pain and heartbreak. But then to believe that it had not been her choice was just too disempowering, too depressing.

"I know that a lot of you right now are thinking – I didn't ask for this. I didn't choose this situation, I didn't want this. But let me assure you – it *was* your choice. And there's no point in worrying about the choices that have led you here. There's no point in berating yourself for making the wrong choices. What you need to realise, is that right now, you have the power to choose what reality you will experience next. Your life is in your hands."

Michelle smiled and took another sip of water.

Natalie glanced around at the people in the room. Most were nodding their heads, some looked as though they had seen the sun for the first time in their lives. Like everything was suddenly illuminated and they could see where they had been faltering, where they had been having problems.

Natalie turned her gaze back to the front of the room and listened intently to the rest of the seminar.

\* \* \*

"So, what did you think?" Evelyn asked as they left the seminar a while later.

Natalie was quiet while she tried to find the words to explain how she felt. "That was, well, for a lack of a better word, illuminating. Inspiring. Everything she said seemed so fantastical, so unbelievable, and yet so sensible and normal at the same time!"

Evelyn smiled. "Most universal truths are very sensible and normal. And believe it or not, each person knows them all. They've just forgotten that they do. So when they're reminded, of course it seems like common sense to them."

"Is that what this dimension is all about then, reminding people of what they already know?"

"Yes, I think that is a perfect summation of what we do

here."

"We? I thought you were the only one who lived here?"

Evelyn nodded. "Yes, I am the only one, but the dreaming volunteers are integral to my job. I couldn't do it without them." She glanced at her watch. "I'm afraid we're late for our next appointment." She held out her hand and this time, when Natalie took it, she didn't close her eyes.

Expecting something incredible, maybe a flash of bright light or something, Natalie was slightly disappointed when all that happened was that the corridor they'd been standing in simply faded away and their new location revealed itself.

She looked around them disbelievingly. "Are we in a supermarket?"

"Yes, my dear," Evelyn replied, reaching for a shopping basket. "Are you hungry?"

Natalie shook her head. "Actually, even though I've been here for-" she cut herself short and frowned. "How long have I been here for?"

"I'm not sure, dear. I'm afraid time hasn't much meaning to me anymore."

"Well, anyway, even though I've been here for a while now, I don't feel hungry. Or tired. Or thirsty. Is that normal?" She followed Evelyn to the fruit section and waited patiently for the answer while Evelyn selected some apples.

"It depends on your idea of normal. In this dimension it is entirely possible to eat, sleep and drink. But is it necessary? No, it's not."

Natalie's eyebrows shot up. "It's not necessary? You mean, you never sleep? Or eat? But how do you survive?"

Evelyn held up a melon. "What do you think of this one? Does this one look good to you?"

Natalie shrugged impatiently. "Yes, it looks fine."

Evelyn sighed. "I realise that you've already had too much

to take in, and that this all must be so confusing to you, but we're not on earth anymore. The reality here is significantly different to the reality of earth. The laws, though similar, are not the same. One of the major differences is that anyone who lives here does not need normal human sustenance to survive. Nor do they need rest," Evelyn's voice dropped. "Though sometimes, there is need to lie down, close your eyes and try to forget what you have seen."

Natalie frowned, wondering what Evelyn had seen that she wanted to forget. Not wanting to pry, she changed the subject.

"So how do you help people in a supermarket?"

Evelyn shrugged. "It depends. Sometimes all people need is a kind word, a smile, or even a little help in selecting the right item."

Natalie randomly picked up some oranges and put them in Evelyn's basket. "And the next person we're going to help will have their life changed if we help them find the right thing to buy?"

Evelyn smiled at the sceptical tone in Natalie's voice. "Remember what I said before? Finding our way in life is really incredibly simple. Which means it sometimes takes a very simple thing to trigger a massive change."

Natalie frowned, still in doubt. "So, when is the next person due to arrive?"

Evelyn glanced at her watch as she deliberated over which cheese to buy. "Not long now. Stilton or Brie?"

"Er, neither. Have they got any mild cheddar?" Natalie asked, suddenly feeling a little hungry.

"Mild cheddar? What's wrong with a little flavour?"

"Flavour is fine, but strong cheese just smells like feet to me," Natalie said as she reached for the mild. "Tastes like feet, too."

Evelyn chuckled and added some Stilton to the basket anyway. She glanced around the empty shop and then looked at her watch again. "Time to set the scene, don't you think?"

Natalie glanced around. "What do you mean?"

Before Natalie had even finished her question, the supermarket was busy and alive with people. Shoppers, shelf-stackers, checkout staff, managers; all looking like they'd been there all along.

Natalie blinked. "How do we tell which one needs help?"

"That's easy," Evelyn replied, moving to the delicatessen counter. "All of the people who have just appeared are dreamers, and if you look at them closely enough, they're slightly blurry around the edges, and are also ever so slightly transparent. Whereas the one we need to help will be much denser, and clearer, like us." She smiled at the deli assistant. "Three slices of ham, some of the cheese pasta salad and some olives, please."

"Certainly ma'am."

Evelyn looked up at Natalie. "Ah, he's arrived."

Natalie looked around. "Where?"

"He's just entered the shop. He's in the newspaper section."

Natalie moved to the next aisle, pretending to look at a loaf of bread. The man wasn't difficult to spot – somehow his clothing and skin colour looked incredibly dull against the bright colours of the supermarket. She noticed his scruffy appearance, his greasy hair and his slumped shoulders.

She went to find Evelyn, who was now sizing up the different breakfast cereals on offer.

"What's wrong with this one?" she muttered quietly.

Evelyn tutted sympathetically. "Bankruptcy. He trusted

his business partner with the financial side, and, needless to say, he messed it up. And so Grant there," she nodded her head to the front of the shop, "lost everything. House, car, possessions, even his girlfriend."

"Ouch. I guess he's pretty low right now then, huh?"

"Just a little. He feels like he's become completely invisible. He hasn't had any real human contact for the last two weeks. He's beginning to believe that if he were to disappear, no one would even notice."

Natalie raised an eyebrow. "How do you know so much about him already? I thought you had to read the aura? You've barely even glanced at him."

"You really are observant, aren't you?" Evelyn nodded happily. "I think you are an excellent replacement for me. Being aware and observant are both very important parts of this job."

"You didn't answer my question," Natalie insisted, trailing after Evelyn to the frozen foods section.

Evelyn smiled patiently as she picked out a bag of peas. "You're right. On many things. I did say that I read people's auras to see their story, to figure out how to help them. But that's actually just how you start out. I told you that, because that's how you will begin, when you take over. But like I also said before, this dimension has its own rules. I've been here for so long now that everything I need to know about a person who needs help, I just know. As clearly and as surely as I know my own name."

"So will I be able to do that one day? Just know everything? Without even trying?"

"I believe so. But then, everyone is different." Evelyn walked slowly toward the checkouts and Natalie trailed behind her, lost in thought.

"Oomph!" Natalie sputtered when she walked into

Evelyn's back.

"Sorry, dear," Evelyn whispered over her shoulder. "But I need you to just stay over here for a moment, okay?"

"Okay," Natalie whispered back, turning to look at something on the end of the aisle. She blushed a little when she realised it was a display of condoms. She randomly picked up a pack and looked out of the corner of her eye as she pretended to read the print on the back.

"Oh dear!" Evelyn exclaimed as some of her shopping fell from her overflowing basket.

Movement caught Natalie's eye as she saw Grant rush forward to help Evelyn. From this angle, because she wasn't looking directly at him, she thought she could see a haze around him. It was a blackish brown colour, darkest around his head and his chest area. She put down the packet she was holding, and picked up another, shifting slightly so she could get a better view.

She saw Grant pick up the shopping, and Evelyn say something to him. Natalie's eyes widened as she saw the haze around him lighten. He smiled at Evelyn and escorted her to the checkout, helping her to place her items on the conveyor belt. Evelyn smiled at him, placing her hand on his arm gently. At her touch, his aura took on a pink tinge and he smiled even more widely. He said goodbye to her, and walked toward the exit of the supermarket without buying anything.

Natalie watched him leave, noticing how his shoulders seemed a little straighter.

"Can't find the right kind?" a voice asked, making Natalie jump. She turned to see a man who was a little blurry with a cheeky smile on his face. When she looked at him blankly, he gestured to her hands. She looked down at the packet of condoms and her cheeks burned a bright red.

"Oh, uh, actually I think these will do just fine," Natalie stammered, backing away from the man.

He chuckled and nodded. "He's a lucky guy," he called after her.

Beyond embarrassed, Natalie all but ran to the checkout and added the packet to Evelyn's purchases. Evelyn raised an eyebrow but thankfully didn't say a word.

Once their shopping was paid for and bagged, Evelyn and Natalie made their way to the exit of the supermarket.

"Why are we continuing the charade?" Natalie asked in a hushed voice. "Why don't we just disappear?"

"You'll see," Evelyn replied, as they reached the automatic doors. Just before they exited, Natalie looked up and saw Grant leaning against the wall, seemingly lost in his own world. Suddenly, as though he felt her stare, he looked at her. Like a deer caught in the headlights, Natalie did what was instinctive to her when someone caught her like that. She smiled.

With a look of surprise, but also delight, Grant smiled back.

# Chapter Eight

As they stepped through the automatic doors, Natalie felt something growing in her chest. It was a feeling that something really quite incredible was happening, she felt as excited as a child on Christmas Eve. So wrapped up in this feeling, she barely noticed that they now stood in the tearooms where she'd first met Evelyn. Evelyn bustled off to the kitchen area, taking the bags of shopping gently from Natalie's grasp. She was setting everything out neatly onto plates when Natalie finally snapped out of it.

"Is this really happening?" she whispered.

Despite being across the room, Evelyn heard her and looked up. Smiling, she crossed the room and enfolded Natalie in a hug.

"Yes, my dear. It is indeed happening." She took her hand and led her over to a table, helping her to sit down as though she were a child. She tucked a strand of Natalie's hair behind her ears, and leaned down to kiss her on the top of the head.

"I know this is a lot to take in, I'm afraid I may have been too rushed in teaching you everything I know." She moved to the counter to get the food. Once the table was set, she eased herself into the chair opposite.

"You have no idea how wonderful it has been, having your company. I have been here many, many years now. And though it will be wonderful to return and live my life, I shall miss you."

Natalie looked up, surprised at the sudden emotion in Evelyn's voice. "How long have you been here?"

"A long time. Since I was about your age, in fact. I had just been dumped by the man I loved, and like you, found myself wandering, lost, with nowhere to go." She brushed a tear from her eye and picked up her fork, gesturing for Natalie to do the same. "I ended up here, in Pam's Tearooms." She smiled, looking around the homey interior. "I've always liked this place."

"And who was here to meet you?" Natalie asked, absentmindedly spearing some pasta on her fork.

"A lady called Edith. Who, I have to admit, bore such a resemblance to my own grandmother that I called her that when I first met her."

Natalie blushed a little, remembering that she had done the same.

"My grandmother had died just a couple of years before. And I missed her dearly."

"So you came here, when you were my age, and you never left? Did the lady, Edith, leave?"

"Yes. She left after showing me all that she knew. And I have been here ever since."

"When was that? In earthly terms, I mean, what year was it?"

"It was nineteen fifty-four."

Natalie's eyes widened. "Nineteen fifty-four? You've been here for fifty-six years?"

Evelyn smiled at her incredulous tone. "Yes, but like I said before, time hasn't much meaning to me anymore."

"But how do you know so much about the earth now? I mean, you don't act like someone from the fifties."

"Well, there's the cinema, of course. I've watched all the movies as they are made, which gives me a great insight into the human race and its progression. I also talk to the dreaming volunteers and sometimes even the people I am helping give me clues to the world and its workings."

Natalie smiled in wonder. Then her eyes narrowed as she considered something. "Will I have to stay here that long? I mean, what if I stay here for fifty years, and when I go back, there's nothing left? Or at least, there's nothing familiar left?"

Evelyn smiled reassuringly. "My dear, didn't you realise from your life review? It doesn't work like that. When you return to earth - which you can do whenever you wish - you re-enter the world at the exact moment before you left it."

Natalie frowned, remembering the part in her film where she drove the car back down the lane and then continued on to meet her husband. "You mean, when I leave, even though I might be here for fifty years, it will be as though no time at all has passed on earth?"

"That's right, yes."

"So when you leave here, you'll become twenty-five again, and go back to nineteen fifty-four?"

Evelyn grinned. "By George, I think she's got it!"

Natalie smiled back. "My grandmother used to say that."

Evelyn patted her mouth with her napkin, hiding a knowing smile. "So, is there anything else that's puzzling you, any other questions you want to ask while we eat this fine food?"

"Actually, there is. I still can't get my head around the idea of no time having passed. I mean, Janet stayed in the hotel for the night, but when she leaves in the morning, she will find herself next to her broken down car, in the previous evening. Doesn't that kind of experience make a person think they've gone mental?"

Evelyn smiled. "It doesn't quite work that way. But I understand your confusion. You see, each person who enters this dimension, when they leave, they re-enter their lives at the moment just before they found the doorway."

"The moment before? So Janet will re-enter her life the moment before her car breaks down? Will her experience in this dimension just seem like a weird daydream then? Or an illusion?"

"Something like that, yes. She may not even consciously remember much of it."

"But then how does that help her?"

"It helps her because though the memory of being in this dimension may be vague, or even missing, the shift that occurs within a person when they are here is as clear as day and stays with them. It is an awakening of their soul, when they remember their purpose and re-discover the meaning of their lives. And that's not something that goes away."

Natalie looked down at her abandoned plate, and nodded. "Okay, I guess that makes sense. Will you remember any of your experience here? Or will you forget it all and wake up in the moment before you came here?"

"Luckily for me, or unluckily, depending on your viewpoint, I will remember most of my life here. Mainly because of my awareness. I know I am in a different dimension, therefore I am more likely to remember it. Just like when you're dreaming and you know it's a dream. In the morning, you are more likely to remember it. Though I'm sure I won't be able to remember every moment, just the highlights, I should think." She smiled at Natalie then stood and picked up her plate. "Did you have any other questions?"

"Wait. You're not going yet, are you?"

Evelyn shook her head. "No, child. But we have much more work to do, and I thought you might want to take advantage of this quiet time." She walked over to the sink and put her plate in it. Then Evelyn picked up the stick of French bread and re-joined Natalie, who had picked up her fork and started eating with enthusiasm. After the first mouthful, Natalie swallowed and sighed.

"This really is the most amazing food I've ever eaten."

"It's amazing how delicious a little imagination can be isn't it?" Evelyn agreed. "Now then, fire away, I know there must be a million more questions in that inquisitive mind of yours."

Natalie thought for a while, her mind running through all of what she had seen and experienced so far. She knew there was something that had been bothering her for a while, something that Evelyn had promised to explain, but she couldn't put her finger on what it was. She ate thoughtfully for a few moments, allowing herself to relax, knowing that it would come to mind, when Mary Beth's lyrics intruded on her thoughts.

"The bar," she said suddenly. She looked up at Evelyn, who was buttering a slice of bread. "Two people 'cancelled' and I didn't know what that meant. You said you'd explain later."

Evelyn shook her head in wonder. "My, my. You really don't miss a thing, do you? Remarkable. I tell you now, your memory will serve you well in this dimension." She held up her hand when Natalie started to speak.

"Don't worry, I am not avoiding the question. It's just not a favourite subject of mine, that's all." She set down the remainder of the bread in her hand and sighed. "When I told you that they had cancelled, what I meant was that it was too late for them."

"Too late?"

"Yes, they had already committed suicide, or brought about their own death in some way."

"Oh," Natalie whispered, dropping her fork onto her plate with a clatter. She had suddenly lost her appetite.

Evelyn reached across the table and rested her hand on Natalie's. "It happens quite often I'm afraid. Far too often for my liking. But then, just as every soul has a purpose here on earth, every soul has the right to choose when they go home. I wish those souls would give life just one more chance, but it was obviously just time for them to go."

"Go home?"

"Yes, my dear. Home. To heaven. Where we have all come from, and where one day, we will all return to."

"Oh. I guess I just never thought of it like that before. Death has always been such an awful thing in my life. I lost my entire family, and all that was left was a gaping black hole in my heart. I guess I always thought that when people die, they just don't exist anymore."

"You couldn't be further from the truth, my dear. The soul lives on after death, I promise you. Your family are all together in heaven, and they are all very proud of you. Especially your grandmother. She has always been proud of you."

Natalie grinned, her feelings of sadness slipping away. She felt her entire being become lighter, brighter. The feeling brought back a memory.

"That was the other question I had for you, Evelyn. What did you say to Grant in the supermarket? I was too far away to hear you properly. It was the strangest thing. I think

I could see his aura. He was surrounded by a hazy blackish brown substance to begin with, but after you spoke to him, it lightened almost instantly. And then, when you touched his arm, it turned to a pinkish colour."

Evelyn clapped her hands together. "That is absolutely marvellous! You are progressing far, far quicker than I ever imagined! Quicker than me, that's for sure. I couldn't see auras properly until Edith left, by which time I had to learn super fast!" She chuckled to herself. "Now then, as to what I said to the young man, Grant, it was very simple. When he picked up my groceries, I simply said 'Bless you, dear, you're an angel.'"

Natalie waited expectantly as Evelyn paused to take a sip of tea.

"Are you going to eat that, dear?" Evelyn asked, eyeing up Natalie's untouched slice of ham.

"What? Oh, no, you go ahead. So what else did you say to him?"

"Nothing. That's all I said."

"But he changed so radically. I mean, not only did his aura change colour, but his whole face lit up, his shoulders were no longer slumped. You must have said more than that, surely."

Evelyn shook her head. "Just some simple words, sometimes it's all you need. Remember, he felt invisible. All I did was acknowledge he existed, and that he was a good person. I have to say, that smile you gave him on the way out, that was definitely the icing on the cake."

"I can't believe that's all it took. I mean, that situation could have happened with anyone, anywhere. It was such a simple incident."

"Simple is best, my dear. Simple, is where the magic is." Evelyn smiled and poured herself another cup of tea from the pot. "So, were there any other questions?"

"Millions. But right now, I can't seem to single out any particular one."

"That's fine, have a little time to think on it, write them down when they come to you."

Natalie nodded and looked down at the table where the notebook and pen from the hotel lay ready. She raised an eyebrow. "Where did they come from?"

Evelyn smiled. "Ask and ye shall receive." She winked.

Natalie chuckled and picked them up, they fit perfectly in her pocket. She pushed her chair back and stood, picking up her dirty plate. She went over to the sink behind the counter and asked over her shoulder: "Does that apply to washing up too?"

Evelyn laughed. She got up and joined Natalie at the sink. "How about I give you a hand?"

"That would be great. Wash or dry?"

*  *  *

As soon as the last dish was dried and put away, Evelyn put the tea-towel down and looked at her watch. She looked at Natalie. "We have an arrival coming up. Are you up for it, or would you like to get some rest, let your mind mull things over?"

Natalie shrugged. "I don't mind. Time to think would be good, but I don't feel like going to sleep or anything. Where could I go?"

"How about the bookstore?"

Natalie nodded, remembering the comfortable arm chairs and hot drinks machine. "Sounds good to me. How do I get there?"

"Just close your eyes, and imagine the bookstore. It may

take a few tries, but you'll get the hang of it."

Natalie nodded and took a deep breath. "Okay, I'll give it a go." She closed her eyes and concentrated on Pam's Bookstore. When she opened her eyes, she let out a squeal of pleasure. She'd managed it on her first try!

"Well done, dear, see you later." Evelyn's voice coming from behind made Natalie jump and spin around. But there was no one there.

"Um, thanks, Evelyn," she replied uncertainly to the empty room. She thought she could hear Evelyn's faint chuckle as she made her way to the drinks machine. She poured herself a hot chocolate, then cup in hand, went to explore.

After only a couple of aisles, Natalie began to believe that perhaps they did stock every book ever written, it was an incredible collection. She selected a few titles and then settled herself at one end of a giant settee. She picked up one of the books, a novel, and turned to the first page. It was an odd habit of hers, but she always felt that when there was too much going on in her life, all she had to do was to lose herself in fiction for a while. It gave her mind a rest and when she emerged from the fictional world, her own world somehow made sense.

It didn't take long for her to completely lose herself in the narrative, completely entranced by the age old story of love, betrayal and reunion. She was just reaching an important revelation in the story when a noise made her jump, and she sloshed her forgotten hot chocolate over the pages.

"Oh, damn," she muttered, looking around for a napkin or tissue to mop up the spillage.

A hand bearing tissues came into her field of vision and she jumped again, spilling more.

"Here, let me take the drink, before it does any more

damage."

"Oh, thanks," Natalie said, exchanging the cup for the tissues. She did her best to salvage the book, but the brown splashes wouldn't come out.

"I guess you'll have to buy that one now, huh?"

Natalie finally looked up at the stranger, and blushed deeply. "Uh, it's okay, I uh, know the owner."

"Ah, that's good. Speaking of which, is she around? There's a book I would like to purchase, but I can't seem to find it."

"Oh, um, could I help you with it?" Natalie asked, setting her books aside and getting up. She ducked her head, trying to hide her still burning cheeks.

"If you could, that would be excellent. The title I was looking for was 'The Beginner's Guide to the Kama Sutra.'"

"Oh," Natalie said faintly, now completely mortified. "I, uh, think maybe, uh, let me go look on the system for you." She forced herself to walk at a normal pace to the counter, but what she really wanted to do was run. Out of all the dreamers in all the world, what was the likelihood of meeting the same one twice? She hit a few random keys on the keyboard, but found that the computer was merely a prop – it didn't actually work. In an effort to calm her raging embarrassment, Natalie closed her eyes, took a deep breath and concentrated on where to find the book.

When she opened them, it was as though someone had drawn a map in her mind's eye. She went back over to the man, who was patiently waiting, still holding her drink. She took the drink from him and set it on the coffee table.

"If you'd like to follow me, I think I've managed to locate the uh, title you were looking for."

"Oh, excellent, thank you."

The walk to the right bookshelf seemed excruciatingly long, but they were finally standing in front of the Relationships section. As politely and as quickly as she could, Natalie muttered her excuses and turned to leave the man to it.

"Thank you, um, what was your name?" the man asked before she could make her escape.

"Oh, uh, it's Natalie," she stammered.

"Natalie. A beautiful name for a beautiful woman. Thank you for your assistance. My name is William."

"Nice to, um, meet you, William. If you have any other queries, just come find me," Natalie replied. She hated herself for saying it, but she was brought up to be polite, and she didn't think Evelyn would be too happy if she was rude to the customers.

Almost tripping over herself in her haste, Natalie hurried away, only breathing easy when she reached the settee again. She picked up the chocolate stained book and continued reading where she had left off, trying to calm herself down so that the red would fade from her cheeks. She soon lost herself again in the story, getting excited, happy, sad and depressed along with the characters. She forgot everything else. All the crazy things that had happened since the moment she stepped through the tearoom door, all the painful things that happened before then, even the two very embarrassing encounters with the man from the supermarket.

All that mattered in that moment was whether Amanda could possibly forgive Marcus for all the awful things he had done to her. Part of Natalie wanted Amanda to stand up for herself, tell Marcus just how much he'd hurt her and that she never wanted to see him again. But another part of her wanted to see them back together. After all, they'd seemed like the perfect couple in the beginning.

Just as the story reached the climax, where Amanda was clinging to life by a thread and Marcus was trying to save her, another loud noise made Natalie jump. At least, this time, she didn't have a drink in her hand.

"I'm so sorry to bother you again, but I was wondering if you were going to be here tomorrow?"

Natalie looked up at William's slightly blurry form, her eyebrows raised in surprise. "I'm sorry?"

"I have to go now, but I was just wondering if you were going to be here tomorrow?"

"Um, I'm not sure, maybe, I guess."

William smiled at her hesitancy. "Excellent. I'll see you tomorrow then."

Natalie nodded shyly and looked down at her book. When she looked back up after a moment, William was nowhere to be seen.

Too preoccupied now to find out if Amanda made it or not, Natalie set the book down and got up, stretching her legs. She wondered where Evelyn was, she seemed to have been gone for quite some time. She wandered around the bookstore, running through the recent events in her mind. It all seemed so unreal, yet at the same time, more real than anything in her life had ever been. She still couldn't believe she'd just been chatted up by a dreamer and she wondered if she should mention it to Evelyn or not.

The question biggest in her mind right then, the main, ultimate question, the one that she needed to answer soon was this: could she really do this? For the next fifty years, maybe even longer, could she live in an alternate universe, helping people in their darkest hour, pointing out the way to those who were lost? She knew that when she returned to earth, she would return to the moment before she left, but that would mean that essentially, she would live two whole lives. One here, then one on earth. She knew she had told Evelyn that she wanted to stay, that she wanted to help people to find their purpose, but part of her was still hesitating to make such a huge commitment.

Her heart ached when she thought about the husband she was going to meet, and the little girl she would have. Could she really wait that long to have the family that she now so desperately wanted? Before, having children wasn't something she had wished for, but watching it happen in her life review had changed that. She'd found the loneliness almost unbearable at home where she lived alone. But here, she would truly be alone, with just dreamers and depressed people to keep her company.

Natalie sighed and ran her hand along the bookshelf she stood in front of. Suddenly, without really knowing why, she pulled a book off the shelf, and opened it, letting it fall open where it wanted. Her eyes were drawn to a passage on the left page, right in the middle.

*There I stood, right on the edge of discovering who I was. There was a fork in the road, and I was free to choose my path. Would I choose to take the unknown path, the one that might open my eyes and help me to realise my true purpose? Or would I choose the safe option, the path that, though tumultuous up until now, was still within my comfort zone? It seems crazy to me now that I did not deliberate longer, that I did not think it through for just a few more minutes. Because if I had the choice to make once more, I would have taken the path of discovery, the path where the outcome was unknown, instead of drowning myself in familiar drudgery.*

Natalie re-read the passage a second time, amazed that she had come across it at this exact moment, when she herself was at the exact same point as the author. She closed the book and silently read the title. *A Life Less Than Lived.* by Natalie J. Wetherby. Her eyes bugged out and she flipped to the back page, where she found a picture of herself. Her photographed self stared back at her, face haggard, eyes full of regret.

# Chapter Nine

"There you are, dear. Have you had enough rest?"

Natalie whirled to face Evelyn, unable to keep the anger from her voice. She held up the book. "Is this some kind of joke? Are you just doing this so that you can escape and imprison me here? I thought it was supposed to be my decision? I thought you said I could leave if I wanted? Are you just trying to mess with my head?"

"Natalie, dear, I promise you, I would never seek to trick you." Evelyn put her hand on Natalie's arm. "I had no idea you would come across that book, and perhaps I should explain this bookstore to you. You see, not only do we have every book ever written, but we also have every possible book that could be written."

Natalie looked at her in disbelief. "Are you trying to tell me that I actually wrote this book, or rather, that I *will* write this book, in the future?"

"Yes, dear. Although it is not certain that you will. Right now, it is still just a possibility. After all, you are in the Possibilities section." She gestured to the sign above their heads, which Natalie had missed earlier.

"Oh," Natalie whispered, looking back down at the book. "So if I choose to go back now, to live my life, I will write this book. But if I choose to stay, and live at Pam's for a while, I won't write this book?"

"It's not quite as clear cut as that, there are so many factors involved, but yes, in short, that is what could happen."

Natalie was quiet for a moment, thinking about the passage she had read, about wishing she could make the decision again, only this time take the unknown path, instead of the familiar one. Right now, that wasn't how she felt. She wanted to go home. Even though there wasn't anyone in particular she wanted to go home to, she felt this incredible longing to be around her possessions, to be where it was familiar. This dimension was incredible, but it was all so much to take in. The things that Evelyn did seemed so complex and difficult. Would she be up to the task?

Evelyn waited patiently while all these thoughts swirled around Natalie's mind.

"Am I allowed to read this?" Natalie asked quietly, breaking the silence.

"Of course, dear. There are no secrets here. Though, whether it would be wise to read it is another matter."

"You don't think I should?"

"My dear, I think you should follow your heart, not your mind. And certainly not anyone else's mind." She patted Natalie's arm and went over to the counter. "Oh, by the way, did William find you?"

"You know William?" Natalie asked in surprise, joining Evelyn at the counter.

"Of course! I know everyone, didn't you know? He was looking for you in the bar. I pointed him in this direction. I hope you didn't mind, dear, but he was quite keen to see you again."

"He came to the bookstore to see me?" Natalie asked, surprised. "But he asked for you…"

Evelyn winked at her. "You must have made quite an impression on him in the supermarket."

Natalie blushed for what seemed like the millionth time. "He's a dreamer, isn't he?"

"He is indeed, and I have to say, I've never seen a dreamer take such a shine to someone before. He must be quite an accomplished lucid dreamer to be able to choose where he goes and who he speaks to."

"Is it difficult to do that?"

"It's not terribly easy, it takes a great deal of concentration and focus. And a strong desire too." Evelyn winked at Natalie.

Unable to take any more embarrassment, Natalie changed the subject.

"So have you had a good, um, afternoon?"

Evelyn shrugged. "It went as well as it could. Have you thought of any more questions for me?"

"Yes, actually, there was something. If I agree to take over from you, and you leave, what happens if I change my mind? What if I want to return to my life in a year? Or in ten years? Will a replacement show up, or will I be stuck here because there's no one else to take over?"

"As I said before, dear, you are free to leave whenever you choose."

"But when I arrived, it sounded like you'd been waiting a long time for me, haven't you been wanting to leave? If you could leave whenever you wanted, why did you have to wait for me to arrive?"

"You really do ask the tough questions, don't you? Yes, I had wanted to leave before you arrived, but I didn't feel like I was waiting impatiently for you to turn up, more like I knew you would appear when I was ready to leave. Everything happens at the right time. Not a minute before or a second after. Therefore, I knew that at the exact moment my soul was ready to return to earth, my replacement would arrive. Fear not, if you choose to leave, then you will not be imprisoned here against your will. At the moment that you are ready to move on, the universe will comply and your replacement will come forth."

Natalie sat down behind the counter, suddenly weary. "It feels like my entire world view has been completely torn apart and reassembled to form an entirely different picture. I'm not even sure how my brain is managing to keep up with all of this. It feels like my time here has been one very, very long day."

Evelyn smiled and sat next to her. "I understand that feeling well. But do you know the best thing to do when your mind feels overwhelm?"

"No, what?"

"Let it go. All those thoughts swirling around, the fears, the questions, the ifs, buts and maybes – all of it. Just let it go."

"How?" Natalie whispered.

"By choosing to. Choose now to let it all go. I think it's similar to what people are calling meditation these days, but I simply like to think of it as just letting go."

Natalie took a deep breath, and closed her eyes. As she exhaled, she imagined everything that was troubling her leaving on her breath as it left her body. Almost instantly, she relaxed and an involuntary smile played across her lips.

"I feel so… free." She turned to Evelyn. "I can't believe it's so simple."

"Well now, you've been here long enough to know that simple is the most magical word in the universe. As the saying goes: 'Life is frittered away by detail… simplify, simplify.'"

Natalie nodded. "I understand what Thoreau meant now.

We get lost in the details, convinced that they matter more than experiencing life as it really is."

"Yes, it's quite amazing to me just how many people sleepwalk through their lives. Who are born, live and die without ever really taking notice of their surroundings. Without ever stopping to notice what's important."

"What is important? What should people be doing?"

"Now that is an interesting question. There is no 'should', not really, because people have free will. They can do as they please. And, as for importance, the only things that are important are the things that feed the soul. The things that make you feel alive, that make your heart leap in your chest at the thought of them."

"What about everything else? The everyday things that we all need to do to survive? Aren't they important too?"

"Necessity does not equal importance."

"But survival is important? Staying alive?"

"That depends on your point of view, my dear. To merely survive is not enough. Surviving is not living. Which is why, though it breaks my heart when it happens, I do believe that for some souls, it is better to depart this earth early than to hang on and 'survive'."

"So it's better to die than to survive, but it's even better to live than to survive?"

"An interesting observation, and indeed, I believe it is accurate."

Natalie sighed. "I think I need to empty my head again, my mind is feeling overwhelmed already."

Evelyn smiled kindly. "By all means, dear, let it go."

Natalie breathed in deeply, then let it out slowly. And once again, she felt better almost immediately. She smiled at Evelyn, her shoulders relaxing a little.

"So what's next? I mean, are there any more places I

should see?"

"We have visited most of the layers in the dimension, but there is just one more that is my absolute favourite. My mentor kept it to last when I arrived here, and I can see why."

"Yeah? Where is it?"

Evelyn smiled. "Seeing as the universe always delivers what is needed at the right moment, there is in fact going to be someone there who may need our help." She held out her hand. "Shall we?"

Natalie nodded and reached out to take Evelyn's hand.

# Chapter Ten

The first thing that Natalie noticed, before she even opened her eyes was the absolute silence. A feeling of stillness and peace stole over her and as she opened her eyes, her breath caught in her throat.

Before her, the scene was majestic. She and Evelyn were sat in a small rowboat, rocking ever so gently on a vast lake which was surrounded by a stunning range of mountains, dark against the sunset streaked sky. For a moment, she just stared at the scene, bathed in a feeling of awe.

"I love it when they choose somewhere stunning," Evelyn whispered.

"Who're 'they'?" Natalie whispered back, unwilling to disturb the silence.

"The creative ones. When they are feeling stuck creatively, whether it's writer's block, a blank canvas or just an inability to see the beauty that surrounds them, they can sometimes find themselves slipping into daydreams where they are somewhere so breathtakingly beautiful, their creativity returns."

"So right now, we're in a daydream?"

"In a sense, yes. This is a place where this particular artist has spent time and where she felt utterly peaceful and still."

"So are we seeing now what she's seeing in her daydream or is she going to turn up here?"

"She should be along in just a moment. For now, let's just enjoy the view."

Without another word, Natalie and Evelyn resumed their silence as they rocked gently on the water.

It could have been an hour later, but was more likely just a few moments later when Natalie sensed the presence of another person in the boat.

She glanced out of the corner of her eye and saw a young woman with her eyes closed, sat between her and Evelyn.

She opened her eyes and a smile lit up her face. She very calmly glanced either side of her and her smile grew wider.

"Evelyn," she said softly, her words like ripples along the water. "It's good to see you again. Who is your friend?"

"This is Natalie. She's my replacement. Natalie, this is Liz."

"Your replacement? Where are you going?"

"It's time for me to return to the earthly dimension. Live my life."

"I wish you the very best, Evelyn. I'll miss our talks." She gestured to the scene before them. "I told you this place was amazing, didn't I?"

"Yes. I understand your attachment to this place now. I don't think I've ever been anywhere that's quite so tranquil."

"Where are we exactly?" Natalie asked, her whisper only slightly louder than theirs.

"We are on the Doubtful Sound, in New Zealand. I came here on holiday a while ago, and I never wanted to leave. Now, when I need inspiration, this is where I come to." Liz smiled sideways at Natalie. "In my mind, of course."

"Are we in the real place right now? Or in your mind?"

Evelyn answered the question. "In a sense, we are in the real place, but not in the same dimensional layer as humans on earth."

Natalie's eyebrows raised at Evelyn's words. "I'm not sure I quite understand what you mean, but I must say, it is spectacular."

"It is," Liz breathed. "I could stay out here forever."

For a few minutes all that could be heard was their soft breathing and the tiny wavelets lapping against the edge of the boat.

"Anything you want to talk about, Liz?" Evelyn asked.

"No, nothing in particular. I just needed to escape." Liz breathed deeply. "Sometimes the constant whirring inside my head gets to me and I just need to get away."

"That's fine, dear. You know where to find us if you do need to talk. Well, where to find Natalie now, I suppose."

"Thank you, Evelyn. I really am going to miss you. You've been an amazing source of inspiration and advice."

"I'm glad I was of help to you, dear. I wish you all the best too. I'm glad that you have somewhere so beautiful to escape to. If only everyone had such an amazing imagination to lose themselves in."

"Yes, I do think the world would be a little less grim if people had somewhere to escape to like this, even if only in their minds."

"But don't people escape every night when they sleep?" Natalie asked.

"Yes, they do. But most don't remember it. When they awake, they have this glorious feeling of freedom for about a minute, then their daily lives intrude and they find themselves slamming back into reality. Whereas a daydream like this one is not only remembered, but can be used as a source of inspiration and motivation."

"So when people daydream or remember a place or an experience, a part of them is really there, like Liz is here now?"

"Yes. I have long believed that a memory is not merely the recall of a moment in the past, but it is in fact the doorway to an alternate reality where that moment is the present."

Natalie smiled at Evelyn's definition. "I don't think I would have believed that before, but now, being here at Pam's, I believe you may be onto something there."

The silence fell again, as the three women sat in contemplation.

Liz sighed softly, and Evelyn smiled.

"Are you sure there's nothing we can help with before you go?"

Liz smiled back. "I'm sure." She reached out and hugged Evelyn. "Thank you. For everything. I hope maybe we will meet again someday."

"I hope so too, my dear. If you do need anything, Natalie will be here."

Liz nodded. She took one last look around, smiled at Natalie, then slowly faded away.

"I didn't know I had made the decision to stay," Natalie said quietly.

Evelyn smiled. "Then you are not listening to your heart, my dear. Listen now, because if you cannot hear it here, you will never hear it."

Natalie nodded. "Will I learn how to read people's minds the way you do? Or, rather, read people's hearts the way you do?"

"Perhaps. We are all unique in the way that we work in this dimension. But I do see some of myself in you, so I think you may discover you have the same talents."

"When do you have to leave?"

Evelyn glanced at her watch. "Soon, dear. Soon."

Natalie nodded. She breathed in the still air, and closed her eyes.

"Would you like a cup of tea?"

Natalie opened her eyes and nodded. She settled herself into the cosy chair while Evelyn bustled around the tearoom kitchen.

"Cake, dear?"

"Yes, please."

Before Natalie had a chance to gather her thoughts, Evelyn was sat at the table, having set a steaming teapot, two cups and two slabs of cherry and coconut cake in front of them.

Evelyn poured two cups of tea, and in silence they each added milk and sugar.

"You knew I would stay, didn't you?"

"No. I knew that you staying was a possibility. It's your choice to stay or not. It's always your choice."

"I choose to stay."

Evelyn nodded. "A wise choice. Now, have you any more questions for me before I leave?"

"You're leaving now?" Natalie panicked a little, she thought she would have more time with Evelyn.

"In a few moments, yes."

"How do I read people's hearts? Their minds? Their auras?"

"By listening to your own heart. In all honesty, there is no question I can answer better than your own heart can. Everything you need to know, you already know. You just need to find that stillness within you to be able to hear it."

"So I guess there's nothing more to ask."

"It would seem so, my dear."

Natalie looked down at the cherry cake she was nibbling chunks of. A sadness washed over her as she realised that this could be the last real human contact she would have in a very long time.

"You won't be alone."

Natalie looked up and smiled. She should have known that Evelyn was listening to her thoughts.

"I will miss you though."

"I will do my best to visit. But right now, I have a life I need to go and live." Evelyn pushed her chair back and stood slowly. Natalie stood too, and felt tears collecting in the corners of her eyes. She bit her lip, and tried to stop them from falling.

Evelyn moved forward and hugged her. "I will see you again, my dear. Until then, know that you are never alone."

Natalie nodded into her soft shoulder, tears now flowing freely down her cheeks, wetting Evelyn's knitted jumper.

"It's time for me to go."

Natalie hugged Evelyn tightly for another moment, then stepped back, wiping her face with her hand. Evelyn handed her a white lace handkerchief with E.M. stitched on it. Natalie took it gratefully then blew her nose and wiped her eyes.

When she focused again on Evelyn, she gasped.

Stood before her was a glamorous young woman in her twenties, dressed in a beautiful nineteen fifties dress, complete with gloves, pearls and perfectly coiffed blonde curls.

"Evelyn?" Natalie whispered.

The young woman smiled, her whole face lighting up. "I'd forgotten what it feels like to be young." She looked down at herself and smoothed out a non-existent wrinkle in the floral fabric. She glanced at the watch on her wrist, which now looked brand new.

"It's time." Evelyn took a deep breath. "Time to live my life." She walked toward the front door of the tearoom. Natalie followed behind, desperately trying to think if there was anything further she needed to say or ask.

Evelyn turned to face her once more. "You will be just fine, my dear." The endearment seemed strange coming from the lips of a young woman.

"Thank you, Evelyn." She swallowed thickly. "I love you," she added in a whisper.

Evelyn nodded, then turned back to the door. With a deep breath she stepped forward and the door opened. A bright light filled the tearoom, making Natalie squint. Through her narrowed eyes, she watched Evelyn step through the door and disappear into the light. The door closed behind her and Natalie was alone.

The silence was as complete as it was on the lake in Liz's daydream. Natalie was at a loss as to what to do. The path she had chosen seemed to stretch out before her, twisting, winding and going in several different directions at once.

Suddenly exhausted, Natalie returned to their table and sat. She took a bite of the cake and chewed slowly.

"I've missed her, haven't I?"

Luckily, Natalie had just swallowed the cake, and she narrowly avoided choking on the crumbs. She looked up at William.

"Yes, she just left."

William moved closer. "Are you okay?"

Natalie tried to smile, but failed. Her face crumpled and William held her while she sobbed.

Somewhere in the middle of her sobs, she realised that though he looked a little blurry round the edges, William felt just as solid as Evelyn had, and that somehow, he had managed to find her again.

Gathering her composure, she pulled back from William and looked up at him.

"Thank you. I'm sorry I got your shirt wet."

William chuckled. "I don't think it really matters here. Are you okay now?"

Natalie nodded, wiping her face again with Evelyn's hanky. "Yes, it's silly really, missing someone so much when I only met them recently. But saying goodbye to Evelyn, well, it was like saying goodbye to my own grandmother." She sighed. "At least I got to say goodbye this time though."

William sat in Evelyn's chair. "So," he said, pouring himself a fresh cup of tea. "What happens now?"

# Chapter Eleven

"Excuse me, are you open right now?"

Natalie looked up and smiled at the woman who had just entered the bookstore.

"Yes, we're open. How can I help you?" Natalie scanned the ragged aura and smiled internally at how easy it had become to read people. Within seconds, she knew the woman's entire life history, knew the reason why she was here at Pam's, and knew exactly how to help her. As she went about helping the woman locate the right book to set her back on track again, Natalie thought about how much she had changed in the time she'd been at Pam's. If she hadn't been keeping a journal, she wouldn't have known how long she'd been there, but earlier she was flipping through the notebook Evelyn had given her, and worked out that she had been there for five years.

Five years. It felt like both a lifetime and a few seconds. She had helped more people than she could count. She had mastered the art of reading their auras, and she could sense who needed help in what layer of the dimension. William had been a great help. He had seen much of what Evelyn had done over the few years he had been helping at Pam's as a dreaming volunteer, and he had helped Natalie on a few occasions in the beginning. Now she was comfortable in her role, he mainly came to visit her to keep her company and to tease her. Nothing had happened between them as such, and Natalie wasn't even sure if anything could. But she was happy just to spend time with him for now.

"Am I interrupting?"

A gentle voice jolted Natalie from her thoughts and she looked up from the books she was shelving. For a moment, she was speechless.

"Evelyn?"

The young woman smiled and nodded at her. Natalie set down the book she was holding and stepped forward. Evelyn held out her arms and wrapped them tightly around her.

"I can't believe it! Where have you been?" Natalie stepped back to look at Evelyn, who seemed to be just a few years older than when she left Pam's as a young woman.

"I've been living! I've met a wonderful man, and we've been having such a lovely courtship."

Natalie smiled. "I'm so glad you've come to visit me."

"I'm so sorry it wasn't sooner, but to be honest it took me a while to be able to direct my dreams in this way. As it is, I don't know how long I can stay. Is everything going well?"

Natalie nodded. "Everything is going just fine. Not a huge amount has changed in the last few years. But I'm getting better at it all, I think. William has been a massive help."

Evelyn glanced around. "Where is he? I'm glad he stuck around a while."

"He should be along soon. Do you want to go to the tearooms for some tea and cake?"

Evelyn smiled. "I'd love to, but I'll probably be woken up

soon, I guess that's one of the joys of motherhood."

Natalie's eyes widened. "You have a child?"

"Yes, I do. A little girl. I adore her, but I must admit, I miss my sleep!"

Natalie laughed. "I bet. Sometimes I go to the hotel, lay in one of the beds and close my eyes for a while, just to feel like I've slept a little."

For a moment Evelyn closed her eyes, when she opened them, she sighed. "I've got to go, I can hear her stirring."

Natalie stepped forward for another hug. "Thank you for coming to see me. Will you be able to come again?"

"I will do my best. Just as you are doing your best here." Evelyn's body started to blur a little more, then began to flicker. "I'm proud of you, Natalie."

Before Natalie could respond, Evelyn was gone.

"Hey."

Natalie felt a hand on her shoulder and she tried to wipe away her tears quickly, but it was too late.

"What's wrong?" William asked.

"Nothing, I'm fine. Evelyn was just here."

"She was? I missed her again. Was she okay?"

Natalie nodded, she bit her lip and willed herself to stop crying but the tears kept falling.

"So why are you crying?" William asked gently, rubbing her arm.

"She has a child. A little girl. Which is why she hasn't visited, she hasn't been getting much sleep."

"That's great. Though it's hard to imagine the Evelyn I knew being young and having a baby. It seems like she was always a grandmother." William peered at Natalie, her tears falling faster now. "What is it? You can tell me." He led her over to the settee and they sat down. She took Evelyn's handkerchief from her pocket and tried to stem the tears.

"When I first came here, and Evelyn was showing me around the dimension, she took me to the cinema where I watched my life. She said it was like a life review. Only, it didn't just go up to the point where I entered the doorway to Pam's, it carried on." Natalie looked up at William. "It's hard to know what the exact timing would be, but I think that if I had returned to earth, by now, I would have a child of my own. A little girl."

William smiled. "Really? I can see that. I think you would make a great mother. You look after everyone who comes here so well."

Natalie nodded, but didn't trust herself enough to speak. After a few minutes of silence, William reached out to touch her hand.

"Nat? What is it?"

"I'm not sure if I can do this. I'm not sure if I can stay here in this dimension for fifty years like Evelyn did. It feels like while I'm helping others to get their lives back on track, my own life is on hold. I mean, I love helping people, I love seeing their faces light up and their auras change from dark to light, but sometimes I get lonely. And I wonder what it would be like, to be with the man I saw in my life review."

William squeezed her hand. "You're not alone, Nat, I'm here. And I'm not going anywhere."

Natalie put her other hand on top of his. "Thank you. You have no idea how much..." Natalie's voice trailed off when she noticed a smooth band of metal under her fingers. She looked up at William. "You're married?"

William nodded. "Yes, I got married last year. I thought you realised."

Natalie withdrew her hands from his. "No, I didn't realise." She stood up abruptly. "I'd better go, there's a soul about to arrive in the supermarket."

William smiled and stood up too. "Ah, the supermarket. I have such fond memories of that part of the dimension." When Natalie didn't respond to his joke, he touched her arm. "Nat? Are you okay?"

"You shouldn't be spending all your time here, with me. You should be with your wife. I'm sorry if I've been keeping you. I thought, well, I thought that maybe we, well, never mind. I think you should go now."

"Hey, slow down, what's wrong? It's not like being with you is cheating on her, I mean, I'm dreaming right now, this isn't really real life."

Natalie bit her lip. To have their relationship described as such hurt, but he was right, in a way.

"It's real to me," she whispered. "And I won't be the other woman. Even if I am in a different dimension to your wife."

William sighed and tried to reach for her again, but she stepped away from him.

"It's really not like that at all, please let me explain."

"There's no need. I think you should go now."

"Nat, please, hear me out-"

"I'm sorry," Natalie cut in. "Goodbye, William."

Before he had a chance to reach out for her again, she closed her eyes and moved to another layer.

Without bothering to open her eyes, Natalie slumped into the seat in the darkened theatre. Sounds of the film surrounded her, loud enough to cover her sobs.

\* \* \*

"Have you figured it all out yet?"

Natalie opened her eyes and smiled up at the soul who had just wandered into the park. She gestured for the soul to join her, and for the first time, absorbed all she needed to know about her without even having to read her aura. She smiled at the woman.

"There's nothing to figure out, all you have to do is close your eyes and listen."

The woman sat next to her, leaned back into the wooden bench and closed her eyes. As she listened to the leaves rustling gently in the warm breeze, Natalie watched the tension, pain, and anger lift from the woman's face. Within moments, she looked younger and more relaxed. Suddenly, a large blue butterfly flew over to them and landed on the woman's hand.

Natalie smiled. It was amazing the effect that butterflies had on people. She came to the park whenever she needed to relax, and there always seemed to be numerous butterflies around, enjoying the beautifully kept flowers. Sometimes she met a soul in need of help, sometimes she just listened to the songs of the wind, enjoyed the view and watched the butterflies.

The woman stirred and opened her eyes. She stared down at the butterfly resting on her hand in wonder, looking even more youthful. "That's amazing," she breathed. "Just now, when I closed my eyes, I asked for a sign that I should move on with my life. A sign that it was time to say goodbye to what I used to know." She stared down at the butterfly. "The day my mum died, a blue butterfly, just like this one, landed on my shoulder, and it was then that I knew she had gone. Sure enough, a few minutes later I received the call to say she'd passed."

The woman took a deep breath, and though Natalie already knew the whole story, she waited silently for her to continue.

"Since then, my life has been one struggle after another.

I just can't get myself on the right path. Nothing has worked out. Not my career, my relationships, or my social life." The woman sighed. "All the way through, I just never stopped for five minutes to consider that maybe I was missing the point. The point of life, the point of anything."

Natalie smiled, thinking of her own life previous to entering Pam's Tearooms. "I know what you mean. It's all too easy to just keep going, regardless, never stopping to think that maybe we're going in the wrong direction."

The woman nodded. "I was just driving along, taking no notice of where I was going, when I saw the signs for this park. I don't know why, but I just had to stop. I've never noticed this place before." She looked from the butterfly still resting on her hand to Natalie. "I'm sorry if I've disturbed you, I'm sure you came here for the peace and quiet, not to listen to me rambling on."

"You haven't disturbed me at all. I'm just glad I was here for you to talk to. Though I haven't done much."

"You have, you told me to stop and listen. Which is something I haven't done in a very long time. I know what I need to do now."

Natalie once again tuned into the woman, sensing her decision, and the path that now lay in front of her. "You've made the right decision. Everything's going to work out just fine."

The woman smiled and lifted her hand, causing the blue butterfly to fly away. She watched it go, then turned to Natalie. "Thank you, that really means a lot to me." She leaned forward and hugged Natalie, taking her by surprise. Natalie returned the squeeze, realising that she had missed having human contact. Her thoughts returned once again to William and she sighed.

The woman pulled back. "What is it?"

"Nothing, I was just thinking that it's time for me to go. I wish at times I could just stay here forever."

The woman looked around at the bright flowers that were surrounded by every different colour and size butterfly imaginable. "I know what you mean. But if we always stay in the same place, how will we ever grow?"

\* \* \*

As Natalie wrote the woman's words down in her notebook later, she found herself thinking of William again. Had she been right to send him away because his heart belonged to another? She wished now that she had thought a little harder before telling him to stay away. She missed his companion-ship, his cheeky smile, the heat of his body next to hers as they discussed the workings of the world.

The years without William had passed so slowly, that Natalie began to doubt whether she would be able to stay in the dimension as long as Evelyn had. She was desperate to have the relationship that she knew was waiting for her, to have the family she had been yearning for. The years had had pretty much erased the memory of the hollow darkness she'd found herself in after Phillip's rejection. But at the same time, she was hesitant to re-enter a world where that kind of pain was possible.

"I'm sorry to bother you, but I'm not sure I'm in the right place."

Natalie closed her notebook and looked up at the middle-aged man standing in front of her desk. "I'm sure you are in the right place, sir. Which course were you interested in?"

"I haven't booked a place or anything, I was just passing by, actually, but the course on fears looked quite interesting. I don't know if you could fit me in at all."

Natalie smiled. "Of course we can fit you in, sir, that's no problem at all. If you just go down to the end of the corridor, that course is taking place in the very last door on your right."

"Do I need to pay now?"

"No, there's no need, sir, today's courses are all free of charge. It's our birthday today, we've been open for twenty years now."

"Oh, wow, that's great. Well, congratulations, and thank you very much."

"You're very welcome, I hope you find the course helpful."

"I'm sure I will." The man smiled, and walked down the corridor. Natalie sensed all of his fear and hoped that the course would at least alleviate it a little. She was glad that he'd had the courage to come inside. It seemed that people of all ages were turning to more alternative forms of therapy and help. The Healing Centre had opened not long after she had taken over the dimension, and had been going from strength to strength ever since. They ran courses, talks, classes and seminars on every conceivable topic. Natalie very rarely visited the church layer of the dimension any more. It seemed that when looking for help, people now preferred a less orthodox approach.

Sensing that the man was to be her last customer of the day, Natalie closed her eyes, out of habit rather than necessity, and left the Healing Centre.

In the bookstore, she found herself wandering up and down the aisles, nodding hello to the dreamers she passed. Without thinking about it, Natalie found herself in the Possibilities section. Absentmindedly, she searched through the shelves for her book. The one she would have written if she had left the dimension twenty years ago. Though she had resisted reading it before, a sense of curiosity pulled at her now. She wanted to know what it would have been like, going back to the real world then. When her fingers came to rest on the slot where it had sat, she frowned. Though there was a book with her name on it, the title and the colour had changed.

"*We are one,*" she murmured, pulling the book from the shelf. On the front cover there was a drawing of the inside of a tearoom, with two indistinct figures sat at a table, drinking tea. She smiled in recognition of herself and Evelyn. She turned the book over and read the blurb on the back.

*A fantastical tale of love lost and then found again through the most extraordinary circumstances. When Natalie walked into a tearoom late one dark night, the last thing she expected to find was salvation while eating cake and drinking tea. Not only did she find peace, she also found the love of her life, and a way to learn all of life's most important lessons, while not wasting a single moment of her life.*

Natalie flipped open the back cover and found a picture of herself smiling radiantly. Though obviously older, her skin was quite smooth, and her eyes sparkled, like a mischievous child's. She read the autobiographic blurb under the picture.

*When she's not writing novels, Natalie J Wetherby works as an Energy Healer in a small village in England. She lives with her husband, James, and young daughter, Marion.*

"James," Natalie whispered. "Marion." She smiled. Marion had been her grandmother's name. She closed the book and held it for a while, staring down at the cover. She heard Evelyn's voice in her mind. She knew she was free to read the book, but would it be wise to?

Figuring it couldn't possibly do any harm, and because her curiosity got the better of her, she decided to let the book fall open to wherever it wanted and then read the first paragraph her eyes settled on.

*After an entire lifetime spent in another dimension, witnessing miracles on a daily basis, it shouldn't have surprised me that when I finally returned to my life on earth, the miracles would continue.*

*It was less than a week after I had returned from the other dimension, my other life, and I was in my bedroom, sorting through my memory box. Though I had always kept my possessions to a minimum, there were some things I just couldn't part with, and over the years, I had taken my memory box wherever I went. It mostly contained old family photos, and letters written by my mother to my father when they first met. At the bottom, I found a photograph of my grandmother and grandfather, during their courtship. My breath caught in my throat when I studied the picture closely, and memories of the last time I had seen Evelyn flooded my mind. The dress, the gloves, the pearls, even the blonde curls were exactly the same. My shocked gaze flew to the flowing script at the bottom of the photograph. 'Evelyn Marion and her sweetheart, Edmund.'*

*My shock was complete. I had never known that my grandmother's first name was Evelyn, or even that back in the fifties she was blonde. All of my memories of Evelyn and my grandmother merged in my mind and I realised that she was indeed the same person. And not only that, Evelyn had actually known when we met, that I was her granddaughter from the future. I clutched the picture to my chest and thanked the universe for giving me that precious time with her. And for giving me the chance to say goodbye properly. It made me so happy to know that she had been proud of me.*

Natalie forced herself to stop reading and closed the book. Just as she had written, her mind was whirling. She knew that Evelyn had reminded her of her grandmother, but the fact that she really was her, just blew her mind. She wondered if the lady before Evelyn had been her grandmother. And if so, did that mean that when Natalie finally moved on, she would be handing the reins over to her own granddaughter? The thought of meeting her future granddaughter was just incredible. She wished that Evelyn had said something though. There was so much that Natalie had still wanted to say to her grandmother. But then, considering how much Evelyn could sense about people, she probably already knew all of what Natalie had to say. If Evelyn managed to visit her again, she would have to tell her that she knew. But seeing as she hadn't seen her for the last fifteen years, she wasn't keeping her hopes up. She looked down at the book, at the image of the two of them sat in the tearoom. She was glad that the previous book had gone and she would not be the haggard-looking person filled with regret. It was comforting to know that, just as she had told the woman in the park, everything was going to be just fine.

She re-shelved the book, and made her way to the counter where the next soul was waiting for her counsel.

# Chapter Twelve

Another ten years passed in a blink of an eye, the passing time changing only the thickness of Natalie's notebook, the lines on her face and the colour of her hair. She hadn't slowed though. Her work at Pam's kept her busy at all times, which meant less time for sitting on her own, lost in thought. Things changed more quickly now, new layers appeared, souls were more open to new opportunities. In fact, it seemed as though many of them were finding Pam's before they had reached the very end of their rope, which was something that Evelyn had hoped for. Natalie wished that she could tell her all the new developments, about all the changes, but she hadn't come back to visit.

Natalie was just about to pour herself a cup of tea when she sensed a soul was in need of her help, but the feeling was a confusing one. It was unlike anything Natalie had felt before. She set the teapot down and closed her eyes.

The lake was still and quiet when Natalie arrived. She breathed in deeply and opened her eyes, knowing exactly where she was from the feeling of tranquillity that stole over her. The mountains were just as majestic as she had remembered.

"Isn't it amazing? I have lived almost half of my life in

this part of the world now, and yet I still have not tired of this view."

Natalie turned to face Liz, half expecting to see the same vibrant, young woman she had once met, only to see a much older version - aged and haggard. Natalie tried to sense her energy but didn't receive anything that made sense.

"Liz! I haven't seen you in so long, are you okay?" Natalie found it hard to disguise her shock at the woman's appearance – surely it couldn't have been that long ago since she sat in this same boat with Evelyn?

"I know, I know, age has not been too kind to me. I tell you, that's what having kids does to you! Of course, the cancer hasn't been too kind either."

"Oh, Liz, I'm sorry. Is there anything I can do?"

"I suppose there must be, otherwise we wouldn't be sat here, would we?"

Natalie smiled.

"The reason you haven't seen me here in such a long time is because I moved here, in real life. I couldn't stay where I was, living a life devoid of colour and life. I moved here, and met my husband. We had three kids, and though it wasn't always easy, the challenge was worth it. Especially when, every weekend, we would get in our boat and sail the sound." Liz looked around, smiling. "It truly is a beautiful place."

"All of that sounds amazing, Liz. I'm so pleased that you managed to make your daydreams come true. But how can I help?" While Liz spoke, Natalie kept trying to read her energy, but she kept getting the same confused patterns. She had never come across it before. It was almost as though-

"I'm in a coma. I've been ill for several years now, and I'm afraid it's finally got me. But for some reason, my body just won't let go. So I thought maybe I should come here and ask you what you think I should do."

The energy pattern suddenly made sense to Natalie. Liz's soul had detached itself entirely from her body. Her soul was fully in this dimension, while her body continued by itself. Usually there were threads of energy connecting the two, but Natalie sensed that these threads had already dissolved. Natalie wondered why she hadn't come across other similar cases before.

"Are you ready to leave?"

Liz nodded. "Yes. I mean, I resisted at first, of course. I didn't want to leave my family, my husband. But now, I think I've accepted it. I just hope that they'll be okay without me." She frowned. "Do you think that's why I can't leave? Because I don't know if they'll be okay?"

"I honestly don't know. I've never come across this situation before, not in all the time I've been here since Evelyn left. And Evelyn never warned me this could happen either."

Liz smiled. "So I'm a unique case then?"

Natalie chuckled. "Yes, you are indeed. The only thing I can think to do is to take you to where Evelyn took me, when I couldn't clearly see the big picture of my own life, or where it was heading." Natalie held out her hand to Liz.

Liz looked at her in surprise. "I can come with you? To somewhere else?"

Natalie shrugged. "I don't see why not. After all, there are no limitations here."

Liz took Natalie's hand and closed her eyes without being told to.

\* \* \*

The smell of popcorn filled their nostrils when they arrived at the cinema. It was fairly quiet, with no queues for tickets. Natalie headed for the ticket counter and Liz trailed behind her.

"Two tickets for Liz's Story, please."

Within minutes, they were settled in the comfortable seats of the cinema's smallest screen.

"I'm not sure I understand what's happening," Liz whispered to Natalie, as the theatre darkened and the screen flickered to life.

Natalie patted Liz's hand. "You will," she whispered back. "Just watch."

\* \* \*

Just as Natalie had suspected, when the review of Liz's life reached the point where she had gone into a coma, it didn't end. It carried on to show how her family coped with her death, which followed shortly after.

Natalie glanced at Liz and saw her rapt expression as she watched the story unfold. Together, they watched Liz's three children grow in their relationships and careers and have children of their own. She watched as her husband was there for each of them when they needed it, and how he made more friends and his own life changed and evolved without her.

Silent tears streamed down Liz's cheeks as she watched what she was going to miss out on. Being a grandmother, retiring with her husband, lazy summer days spent on the lake.

Natalie wondered if it had been a good idea, bringing Liz here, was this what she needed to be able to move on, or would this make her cling even harder to the body that wouldn't give up?

On the celebration of Liz's husband's eightieth birthday, the screen faded to black. The lights came up and Natalie handed Liz a tissue.

"Are you okay?"

Liz nodded, wiping her face and blowing her nose. She took a few deep breaths before trying to speak.

"They're going to be okay. That's all I needed to know."

Natalie smiled in relief.

Liz turned to Natalie. "I'm ready to go now, but I'd like to see the sound one last time."

Natalie nodded and held out her hand.

\* \* \*

Back in the tearoom, later on, Natalie wrote down her experience with Liz on the sound. It felt like an important change had taken place. Perhaps now, she would help more souls to move from the earthly plane to the next. She had spent so long trying to help people to stay alive, that it hadn't occurred to her to help those who were ready to move on.

Death had always been such a scary concept to her. She had lost her whole family, how could she not fear it? But today had changed her viewpoint. Liz hadn't been afraid of dying, she had simply been afraid for those she had left behind.

Natalie wondered if that was how her own family had felt, the seconds before they left. Had they been afraid for her? She hoped that wherever they were they knew she was okay. More than okay. Despite the feelings of loneliness that crept in during the quiet moments, Natalie finally felt like she had found her calling. That she had found her place. If she remembered nothing else, she hoped that when she did finally leave Pam's to resume her life, she would remember the feeling of belonging that she felt now.

Natalie took a sip of tea and reviewed her notes. It had been very peaceful, helping a soul to move on from earth to the afterlife. She wondered what would have happened to Liz's soul if she hadn't been there to help her. Would she have just remained in a coma indefinitely? Or would her body have given up eventually, her unrested soul left in the middle dimension forever? Maybe there was a way for humans to help souls move on from the earthly plane. She wrote these thoughts down too, making a mental note to look in the bookstore for any books related to the subject. Perhaps it was something she could pursue when she returned to her life.

Natalie set her pen down and sighed. Her life. It hadn't been much when she left it. She couldn't help but wonder if she would ever feel ready to go back. Back to a world that was changing so rapidly, and not always for the better. Back to worrying about working, paying the rent and keeping up with bills. Having to eat, sleep and do all the domestic chores that came with having your own place. Was it really worth it? Would she be able to remember all that she'd learned here and the peace that she felt now? She thought back to when she had lived with her grandmother. She wondered why Evelyn had never told her about this dimension. Did she have no recollection of her life here, of the times they had spent together here? She recalled the serene smile on her grandmother's face as she baked her famous cakes and cleaned the house. She must have surely remembered some of it.

Natalie sipped more tea. One thing she knew for sure was that when she did go back, her life would be better. The smiling photo in the back of her book told her that much. She knew that she would be a writer and a healer.

But that didn't mean that she wouldn't have struggles, and experience pain and heartbreak. Would the joys of finding a partner and having a child outweigh the challenges that came with being human?

Natalie hadn't asked Evelyn what would happen if she just never returned to earth. Was it even possible not to return? The world was continuing on as normal, so if Natalie never returned, until the end of civilisation, did that mean that she would have simply vanished that night she drove down that lane and found the tearoom? Would she be breaking some kind of universal law by remaining here? Or was it already decided that she was going to return?

Natalie figured there was no way of knowing for sure. She would just have to wait.

* * *

If she had been surprised by the speed of the changes during the previous ten years, then the next twenty years completely blew Natalie's mind. She tried to keep comprehensive notes, in the hopes that they would help the next person to adjust quickly to the environment.

When she had begun her journey at Pam's fifty years before, things had moved at a slower, more leisurely pace. But now, Natalie didn't even have time to rest as she tried to keep up with the near-constant stream of souls who were in need of finding their true purpose and the meaning of their lives.

In a rare moment of quiet, Natalie went to the tearoom, and made herself a cup of tea. Though food, drink and rest were entirely unnecessary at Pam's, the ritual of making and drinking tea reminded Natalie of Evelyn and made her feel like an ordinary human being again. If only for a few minutes.

"No cake today?"

Natalie became still, and closed her eyes. It had been a long time, but the energy was still achingly familiar.

It was only when he was sat opposite her that Natalie allowed herself to look.

"William," she whispered. He was older, that was certain, but the gentle lines and silver grey hairs just made him look more distinguished and, Natalie hated to admit, even more attractive.

"I know it's been such a very long time, but I had to see you."

Natalie frowned. "Why? Why is it so important to see me now?" Despite her slightly cold tone, every part of her longed to touch him, to kiss him. She struggled to keep her facial expression neutral.

William also seemed to be struggling with something. "I can't tell you why." He reached across the table to take Natalie's hand. "I can only apologise for staying away for so long. I wasn't even sure if I would still find you here. I thought you might have moved on by now."

Natalie was silent. She didn't know why he had returned, and part of her didn't care. She didn't pull her hand away from his, it felt too good. But she didn't know what to say.

William took her silence as a negative, and pulled away. "I'm sorry. I just... missed you. I needed to see if you were okay. But I shouldn't have bothered you, I'm sorry."

He pushed his chair back and stood. He was halfway to the door when Natalie finally spoke up.

"Don't go."

It was barely more than a whisper. But it was enough to stop William in his tracks. He turned slowly.

"What?" he whispered back, hardly daring to breathe.

It seemed like an eternity as he waited for a reply. Natalie finally stood and walked toward him, her gaze fixed on the floor as she moved.

She reached him and wrenched her gaze upwards to meet his.

"Don't go. I missed you too."

William didn't waste another second. He stepped forward and wrapped his arms around her. Natalie felt all her loneliness disappear into their embrace.

*   *   *

William stayed for a long time, content to listen to Natalie as she recounted some of the more memorable moments she had experienced since she saw him last. She wondered briefly why he was sleeping for so long, he must be having the longest dream ever. But she didn't linger too long on that thought - she was just glad he was there. She hadn't realised until he'd returned just how much she had missed his company.

They were just pouring their fourth cup of tea when Natalie became aware of an imminent arrival. She really didn't want to ask William to leave, but she could sense that this soul was in great distress, and would need a lot of attention.

"William, I'm sorry, there's someone coming."

Used to the drill, William stood quickly, "No need to explain, I'll let you get back to work."

Natalie stood and he pulled her into a quick embrace.

"I love you," he whispered into her hair, before vanishing.

Natalie blinked, surprised by his admission, and surprised that she felt the same way. If only she could have told him before he left.

Knowing she only had a few more moments, Natalie pulled herself together while clearing away the dirty dishes. Having such close contact with William had unsettled her slightly, but it had also made her realise something.

She was ready to go back. She was ready to experience a relationship for real. She was ready to live her life. Hearing the tearoom door open behind her, Natalie took a deep breath and smiled, pushing all of her thoughts to the back of her mind. She turned to greet the soul but the words stuck in her throat.

# Chapter Thirteen

Emma Poole was in shock.

She generally considered herself to be a lucky person. Her life had been fairly easy so far. She'd had loving, doting parents who had given her just the right balance of love and support. They had helped her to become strong and independent, yet were always there when she needed them. She had the best grandparents (on her mother's side, anyway) who had spoiled her rotten over the years. She was intelligent, good looking and had a positive attitude.

Which was why this had come as such a shock to her system. Her whole life, seemingly picture perfect one moment, had become a complete nightmare the next.

She was completely unaware of her surroundings. The sounds merged into a drone, her vision blurred and her mind blocked everything out except for one thing.

Her parents were dead.

Emma hadn't lost anyone she was close to before. Her grandmother on her dad's side had passed away several years earlier, but she hadn't been close to her, so it hadn't had much impact. She'd never lost a friend, cousin or even a pet. Death just hadn't played any part in her life before. Was that why it was hitting her so hard now? Because she had got off so lightly before?

The loss of both her parents was just too much for her to comprehend. They'd been there just that morning, visiting Emma at her flat on the edge of the city centre. She'd only moved there a few weeks before, and they'd come to make sure she was settled in. Her mother had fussed about, cleaning things, moving things around. Her father had sat on the small settee and had shaken his head at his wife's antics. He'd whispered to her afterwards: "Don't worry, you can move it all back when we're gone."

They'd always been close, her and her dad. They'd hide away in the garden when her mother went on a cleaning rampage. They'd always find something to do: re-potting plants, weeding the flowerbeds or even just sitting behind the shed, talking. Emma remembered running through the house giggling as her muddy boots left tracks all over the recently cleaned cream carpets.

"Emma?"

Her mind was shrouded in fog. Emma blinked, and tried to concentrate on the voice calling her name.

"Emma, sweetheart, are you okay?"

Emma blinked again and forced her eyes to focus on the face in front of her. Her grandmother's features slowly came into focus, a strained, concerned smile on her lips.

With herculean effort, Emma nodded in response, unable to form any actual words. She looked around and saw her grandfather standing at the window of her tiny flat, staring out into the darkness. It surprised her slightly that it was already dark. When that had happened, she wasn't sure.

"Would you like to come and stay with us for a little while, sweetheart?"

Emma blinked yet again, seemingly unable to think coherently. She didn't want to stay with her grandparents.

She wanted to turn back time to the moment that her parents left her flat that afternoon.

"Now, make sure you eat properly, okay, and clean the toilet at least once a week - more if you can. Oh, and you should also clean the-"

"Mum," Emma had interrupted. "I promise to clean. All the time. Every day." She caught her dad's eye and tried not to smile. He knew she was lying just to get her mum to shut up.

"Come on now, Marion, we should get going, we don't want to get stuck in the rush hour traffic."

Her mum had nodded then, and looked at Emma with a look of concern that only a mother could pull off.

"Are you sure you're okay here on your own?"

Emma had smiled at her, in what she'd hoped was a reassuring way. "Of course, Mum. I'm fine."

"Okay, then, we'd better get going."

"Call me when you get home," Emma said, sounding more like the parent than the child.

"We will," her dad promised.

It was the only promise he had ever broken.

"Emma?"

The sound of her name spoken in the present brought her back yet again, only this time she shook her head in response.

"No, I think I'd rather stay here," she managed to say, her voice hoarse with unshed tears. As much as she loved her grandparents, she needed to be by herself. She needed to process what was happening.

Her grandfather moved into her line of vision, slowly kneeling on the floor in front of where she sat huddled on the settee.

"Are you sure, sweetie pie? We don't like to think of you

here all by yourself."

"I'm sure. Thank you. I just need to be alone."

A look was shared between her grandmother and grandfather. They had a way of communicating without speaking. Emma had asked once, how they did it, and her grandmother had answered with some vague explanation about knowing each other before they met. Something about dreams, which Emma didn't understand at the time, and couldn't even begin to comprehend now. Her grandmother glanced down at her watch, then nodded at Emma.

"If you're absolutely sure, sweetheart."

It took a further half an hour before they finally left. Hours later, Emma was still sat on the settee, staring blindly at the carpet.

Another few hours later, she had yet to move, or even to shed a tear.

It wasn't until the room began to lighten in the early morning sun that she moved. Her eyes were drawn to the window, where the noise of traffic was increasing, and the sky was lightening by the second. When moving her gaze back to the spot on the carpet, a photo frame on the coffee table caught her attention, snapping her out of her daze for a moment.

As she stared at their happy, smiling faces, a moment was all it took for her defences against this unthinkable situation to break down.

Oblivious to anything else, Emma collapsed onto the settee and cried until she had no tears or energy left.

It was only then that she slept.

* * *

The following few days passed in that same foggy daze.

Emma did all that was expected of her, as the only daughter. She helped to arrange the funeral, and tried to notify all the family and many friends that her parents had had.

The funeral was overwhelming. Emma had no idea that her parents had known so many people. They'd had fairly normal, somewhat boring lives, Emma thought, but obviously their compassion and caring (despite her mother's tendency to be a bit neurotic) had obviously touched many, many people.

Emma stood between her grandparents, glad to have close family to lean on when she needed it. But she also knew that soon she would have to be strong, and be even more independent than she already was. Her grandparents were getting older, and her grandmother had a heart condition, which wasn't being helped in the slightest by the recent events. Emma needed to brace herself for the inevitability of being completely on her own quite soon.

Back in her flat after the funeral, Emma sat holding the framed photograph, taken only weeks before. Her mum had insisted on recording the occasion when Emma got her first home. Though she was now twenty-five, it was quite young to get her own place, especially on her own. Property prices were so crazy that most young people stayed living at home until they got married. Emma had been saving for years, and with her parents' and grandparents' help, had finally saved enough to buy her own flat. Of course, now that her parents were gone, their house and everything had been left to Emma. Suddenly she found herself with two properties and more money than she had ever seen.

Emma couldn't even contemplate sorting out her parents' home. She had told her grandmother that she would do it in a few weeks, when she had more time to come to terms with everything. Also, she had run out of days off for the time being. Her boss was very understanding, but she was needed back at work. And if she was honest, Emma herself needed to go back to work, it would give her mind and heart a rest from the grief that was, at this moment in time, suffocating her.

A loud buzzing noise knocked Emma out of her reverie, causing her to jump up, dropping the frame. Luckily it fell onto the carpet, no damage done. Emma hurried to pick it up, setting it carefully on the coffee table before answering the door.

"Richard!" she said in surprise. "What are you doing here?"

Richard brought his hands to the front, revealing his grease-stained cardboard-boxed offering.

"I figured you wouldn't be up to cooking, so I thought I'd bring you some dinner."

Emma smiled for the first time in the last week.

"You know me too well, come in."

Richard went past her, squeezing her arm as he went. Emma locked the door and joined him in the tiny kitchen. He'd already got plates out, and had poured two glasses of red wine.

"Found the bottle in the cupboard, thought it might be a good idea, medicinal purposes, of course."

Emma nodded and watched him as he efficiently separated two slices of pizza and set them on the plates. Feeling slightly useless in her own home, she took the glass and pizza offered to her and went back into the lounge. She set the glass on a coaster, remembering suddenly the day her mum had given the set to her, reminding her to always use one so that she didn't ruin the coffee table. The fact that the coffee table had been bought from a junk shop and already had a hundred ring marks on it had completely escaped her mum's notice. Emma had bought it in the intention of rubbing down the wood and painting it cream, to match the rest of the décor. But like most of Emma's restoration plans, it had yet to happen.

"Emma?"

Emma blinked and looked up at Richard, who was obviously wondering why she was staring at her coaster with such intensity.

"Sorry," she said, her voice hoarse. She cleared her throat and tried again. "Sorry, just got lost in my thoughts for a moment."

Richard smiled. "That's cool." He took a bite of his pepperoni pizza, wiping the grease that trickled down his chin with a piece of kitchen towel.

They ate in silence, punctuated only by the clink of the glasses against the glass coasters. When they finished their first slices, Richard got up without a word and got them both another, which they also ate in silence.

Though she appreciated the thought, and the company, Emma knew Richard was probably feeling incredibly awkward. It always seemed like people just didn't know what to say in such a situation. And why should they know? If they'd never experienced it, then they'd have no idea what it felt like.

Emma wasn't entirely sure she knew what it felt like either. Aside from her breakdown the morning after the accident, she had held herself together remarkably well, even at the funeral, when she was surrounded by people crying.

The truth was, she just couldn't accept that they were really gone. She wouldn't. Her grandmother had brought her up to believe in the afterlife, and in souls surviving past the life of the body. So in some way, Emma knew that somewhere, in some dimension, some reality, her parents were still alive.

She had to believe that, because if that wasn't true, then there would be a deep black hole in her heart that would never heal.

It was a while before she noticed that both the pizza and wine were gone, and when she did, she also realised that she was slightly tipsy. She blinked at her friend, who was watching her carefully. She tried to speak but it came out slightly slurred.

"Risshard? Why did thaay haff tuh go?"

The last thing she remembered before the blissful darkness was his arms reaching out toward her.

# Chapter Fourteen

Before she even opened her eyes, Emma could feel the familiar pounding of a severe headache. Carefully, millimetre by millimetre, her eyelids rose upwards, and through the tiny slits she surveyed her surroundings.

She was in her bedroom, under the covers and the blinds were open, letting in the early morning sunlight. Though it hurt to, Emma frowned. She had no recollection of how she'd come to be in her bed. The last thing she could remember was the funeral. Then what? She'd come home, she remembered that.

While scanning her memory frantically, Emma slowly eased herself up into a sitting position, and two things happened at once. The first thing she noticed was a piece of paper under the hand she'd used to push herself into a sitting position. The second thing was that when the cover fell down, she realised she was naked.

Eyes now wide open, despite the pain of the light hitting her headache, she held up the piece of paper and blinked furiously in her attempt to read the words scrawled on it.

'Hey Emma, Last night was fantastic! Sorry I had to leave early, have to be in work by eight. I'll give you a call later, Richard.'

Heart hammering in her chest, the last fragments of Emma's memory resurfaced. Richard at her door, the pizza, the glasses of wine. Then finally, her collapsing into his arms. But then what? She read the note again, her disbelief and anger rising up, making her head pound harder. When he said the night before had been fantastic, there's no way he could have just been referring to the food and wine. And the conversation hadn't exactly been flowing either. Emma looked down at her naked body and it was then that she realised that in her greatest hour of need, one of the people she had trusted implicitly had betrayed her in the worst way possible.

It took all her strength to make her way to the bathroom, and after emptying her stomach, she crawled into the shower cubicle and turned the water on as hot as she could stand it. Her head immersed in the rushing water, she was oblivious to the calls that her answering machine was picking up.

Her mind was stuck on one thing. How could he? How could he take advantage of her when she was obviously in a huge amount of pain and distress? She had just buried her parents only hours before and he saw that as his way into her bed?

She retched at the thought of what he had done to her while she was unconscious. She couldn't believe that she had trusted him! They had been friends for years and though she knew that in the past he had been attracted to her, she had no idea he would stoop this low.

Shaking with anger at herself for being so trusting, Emma ripped her flannel from the hook above her and began scrubbing at her body, desperate to remove all traces of where he might have touched her.

An hour later, exhausted, spent and shivering from the icy cold water that was now falling on her head, Emma got out of the shower and wrapped herself in her favourite towel. Still dazed and headachy, she went into the kitchen to get some paracetamol and water. The pizza box from the night before was still sat on the counter and suddenly angry again, she grabbed it and shoved it into the kitchen bin. She did the same with the napkins and even the plates and wine glasses. She made a mental note to put the rubbish out later. She wanted no reminders of the night before.

Her moment of frenzy over, the blinking red light on the answer machine caught her attention. Glass of water and paracetamol in hand, she went over to the machine. There were five messages. Unsure if she really wanted to hear them, she pressed play.

"Hey babe, just wanted to say how much I enjoyed last nigh-"

Hand trembling, Emma hit the delete button before he could finish his sentence. The next message began.

"Emma, sweetheart? I hope I haven't woken you, just wanted to make sure you're okay, please give me a ring later, love you." Emma's face crumpled at the sound of her grandmother's sympathetic voice and she began to cry quietly.

"Emmy? It's Rachael. I know you probably don't want to talk to anyone right now, but if you do need to, I can come round to yours any time, or you can ring me. Just know you're not on your own, honey, okay? Bye." Emma took the two paracetamol, slugging the water back.

"Hey, Emma, it's Richard again, did I leave my wallet there, I can't seem to-" Again, before he could finish his sentence, Emma cut him off. She glanced around the lounge and saw a brown leather rectangle sticking out from underneath the settee. Shuddering, she couldn't bring herself to go and pick it up.

"Emma? Sandra here. Just thought I'd check to see how you're doing. I've sorted out your workload, and we'll be fine without you for another week. So rest up, look after yourself, and then come back when you've cleared your head okay? Speak soon, bye."

Emma listened to her boss's voice, hearing the sympathy in her tone under the seemingly cold words. Rest up, look after herself and clear her head? Sandra made it sound like she'd had a nervous breakdown, not just lost both her parents. But Emma knew she meant well. Though extremely tough and organised, Sandra was the fairest boss Emma had ever had.

Long after the messages had finished, Emma stood, staring at the machine, its red light no longer blinking. It took a lot of effort to return to her bedroom, where she surveyed the mess. After throwing on her sloppiest jeans and a faded t-shirt, Emma started to strip her bed of the pink sheets that she had bought only weeks before. She'd been so excited to get all new bedding for her new flat, but now, she wouldn't care if she never saw them again. In fact, after washing them, she decided to donate them to a charity shop. She pulled out some old sheets she'd brought with her from her parents' house to put on her bed instead.

Once her room was back in some semblance of order, Emma moved onto the lounge, putting the colourful glass coasters carefully back in their box in the centre of the coffee table. Against her own will, her gaze travelled downwards to the leather wallet. Unable to stand it taunting her, she reached down and picked it up.

She wondered if it had really fallen out of his pocket, or if he had planted it there so he would have to come back to her flat to collect it. The idea of him coming back made Emma feel physically ill. Without stopping to think her actions through, she strode over to the window, and flung it open. She held the wallet outside, and dangled it for a second above the pavement three stories below.

Through her daze of pain and grief, she felt a glimmer of satisfaction when it hit the pavement. When a kid came along and picked it up, pocketing the cash before dumping the wallet in the nearest bin, Emma smiled.

\*   \*   \*

Hours later, Emma sat huddled on the settee, under a thread-worn patchwork quilt her mum had made her when she was a child. Unable to bear the sound of the phone ringing, and the messages people were leaving, Emma had plugged her headphones into her ears. She played her music so loud that it was difficult to focus on anything other than the words of the songs. Whenever the random shuffle hit a slow, sad song, she would press the skip button until a loud rock tune came on.

In a two second lull between songs, Emma heard the buzz of her door bell. Frozen in place, Emma closed her eyes and listened to the next song, hoping that the person at the door would give up and leave when they got no answer.

In the next break, her hoping was shattered by the sound of someone's fist hammering against the wooden door.

Slowly, Emma pulled the headphones from her ears and stood. Feeling a little dizzy from lack of food and drink, she paused for a moment to let her head stop spinning. The pounding on the door got louder. And in between the pounding, she heard her name being called.

Her breath caught in her throat when she recognised Richard's voice. She considered not answering, but knew that he wouldn't give up that easily. Knowing now what he was capable of, he'd probably play the concerned friend card and get the police out to knock the door down, on the pretence that he was worried about her.

She moved slowly toward the door and stopped about a foot away.

"What do you want?" she called out, hating how vulnerable her voice sounded.

The pounding paused for a moment.

"Emma? Are you there?"

"What do you want?" she repeated, a little louder and stronger this time.

"It's me, darling. It's Richard. Didn't you get my messages? I think I left my wallet here last night. Can I come in?"

"You didn't. I've looked everywhere, and it's not here," Emma lied.

"Oh, are you sure? Can I come in and look myself?"

"Why? Don't you trust me?" Emma tried to keep the hysteria from her voice as she tried to figure out how to get rid of him.

"Of course I trust you, darling. I was just certain that I'd left it here."

You're certain because you left it here on purpose, Emma wanted to reply

"Are you okay?" he called out, breaking the silence. "I'm sorry I had to leave so early, I had to go home and change for work. You looked so peaceful, I didn't want to wake you to say goodbye."

Fighting the urge to retch again, Emma stayed silent, tears pricking at her sore eyelids.

"Darling, please let me in. Why won't you open the door? I know you're having a tough time at the moment, but what happened last night, well, it's natural to want comfort when you're grieving. You mustn't feel guilty about it."

Emma's eyebrows raised almost to her hairline as she listened to him. How had she never noticed before what a sleazeball Richard was? He'd got her drunk, probably drugged her and then raped her while unconscious, and yet he had the gall to tell her not to feel guilty about it? It was just too much. All of her anger, her grief and her sheer disbelief at his behaviour exploded out of her suddenly.

"Go away!" she screamed. "I never want to see you again! If you ever come back I'll call the police!"

"Emma? What are you talking about? What did I do?"

"You know exactly what you did, you bastard! Now go before I have you arrested!" A sob escaped from her and she shook with anger, tears streamed down her face.

"I don't understand Emma, why are you being like this?"

"I'm going to count to ten, if you're not gone by then, I swear to God, I will call the police." She held her breath and began to count to ten in her mind.

After five, she heard Richard shuffle his feet, then she heard his voice, much closer to the door and clearer than before.

"You'll never prove I did anything wrong, you slut."

Another second later, she heard his footsteps getting further away down the carpeted hallway.

Completely drained, Emma sank to her knees on the floor where she stood and sobbed.

The phone continued ringing all day.

\* \* \*

"Sweetheart, I know it seems like everything is going awfully wrong right now, but please, please know that it won't last forever. You will get through it, I promise."

Emma smiled at her grandmother. "I know, Gran. You tell me that all the time. And you're right, of course, it's just not so easy to remember that when I'm feeling down. But I do try."

Emma's grandmother patted her on the knee, then turned to look at the beautiful park that surrounded them. Emma turned to look too, amazed at the vibrant colours of the trees and flowers. The sky was the most incredible shade of blue.

"Where are we, Gran? I don't think I've been here before."

Her grandmother smiled. "We are somewhere that's very special to me. One day you will understand. One day soon, if I remember correctly."

Emma frowned, puzzled. "Wait a minute though, is this even real? I mean, am I dreaming? Because everything seems so vivid, so beautiful."

"What is real? What is reality? Why is it that if something is extraordinarily beautiful, it couldn't possibly be real?"

Emma smiled. Her grandmother always liked to answer her questions with more questions. "You're right," she agreed softly. "Besides, real or not, I'm just happy to be here with you, Gran. I love you."

For a second, Emma thought she saw a flicker of pain cross her grandmother's face.

"I love you too, my sweetheart. Come here," she held her arms out and Emma folded herself into them, feeling completely loved in her grandmother's embrace.

A large blue butterfly landed softly on Emma's knee, and they watched it for a few moments before it flew away.

"Tell your granddad I love him too," she whispered into Emma's hair. "With all my heart and soul."

* * *

The cold, hard floor was a shock when Emma's eyes flew open suddenly. She could still feel the warmth and softness of her grandmother's arms, still see the bright, vivid colours of the park, and the shape of the butterfly on her knee. She pushed herself into a sitting position, her muscles screaming from sleeping on the laminate floor in her hallway.

Slowly, she stood up and the dream faded a little, allowing her memory of the previous couple of days to flood her mind. Legs shaking, she made her way to the kitchen, and made herself a strong cup of tea. She considered something stronger, but her stomach turned as she remembered what had happened with Richard. She vowed never to drink wine again.

After a few sips, she began to feel a little better, and she moved slowly to the lounge. The red light on her machine was blinking again. Emma vaguely recalled the phone ringing, perhaps that was what had woken her?

She hesitantly went over to the machine, clutching her cup like a security blanket. There were eight messages. With a shaking finger, she hit play.

"Emma, it's me again, sweetheart, you didn't call me and I'm getting worried. Your grandfather and I just want to know you're okay. We know it'll take some time to heal, to get through this, but we're here for you, okay? Please keep in touch. Love you."

"Emma? It's Sammy. Are you there? Please pick up. I don't like to think of you sat there on your own. If you don't call me back today, I'm coming over straight after work tomorrow to check on you. Okay, well, I'll see you then."

"Emma, it's Richard, you haven't called, so I'm coming over to get my-" Emma cut Richard off, not wanting to hear his voice. She wondered briefly if she should have called the police, but what would they do?

The next two messages contained just a few seconds of muffled sound before the person hung up. Emma deleted them.

"Emma, it's me again. I'm really sorry to keep calling you, sweetheart, but there's something I need to tell you. Something I've been wanting to tell you for years. It's time now. I think it will help you right now. Please call me. Love you."

Emma frowned, her grandmother sounded so, well, serious. She wondered what it could be. The next message stopped her musings and chilled her to the bone.

"You filthy little bitch. I know you've got my wallet. I'll get it from you, even if I have to break down your door to get it. You won't call the police, because if you do, you'll be joining your parents a lot sooner than you planned."

Emma swallowed hard, and was about to hit the delete button when the next message started.

"Emma? It's your grandfather. I'm afraid I have some terrible news, it's, it's your grandmother." Emma's eyes widened as she listened to her grandfather break down on the answer machine. He sobbed for a few moments then rasped, "Please call me." Emma grabbed her phone and frantically dialled her grandparents' number. It seemed to ring for an age before it was answered.

"Granddad? What's wrong? What is it? Is Gran ill?"

There was silence, broken only by the sound of a loud clock ticking in the background.

"I'm sorry, Emma, but she's gone."

Emma's heart thudded hard, once, then stopped still.

"Gone?" she repeated, hoping she had heard wrong.

"She died last night, in her sleep," her grandfather

whispered.

Emma shook her head frantically, "No, no, she can't have, she just left me a message, I just heard her voice, she can't be gone, she can't."

"She rang you yesterday, sweetie pie. Twice, I think."

Emma stared down at the machine, her eyes filling up.

"She can't be gone," she repeated, desperate now.

"I'm sorry, sweetie, I really am."

\* \* \*

So many people. Many of them she had seen at her parents' funeral, just a week before. But if she'd thought there'd been many mourners then, she had yet to see the true spectacle. Most of the faces Emma didn't recognise. But once the seats in the Spiritual Centre were full, more people waited outside, only coming in at the end of the service to pay their last respects to her grandmother, who lay as though she were napping in her lavender lined coffin. It reminded Emma of the scene in the classic film, Evita, where lines of mourners filed past Evita's coffin to say goodbye. Emma hadn't realised how many people had loved her grandmother.

She had worked for many years as a healer and a medium, and even wrote several books on the subject. Emma had never read them. As much as her grandmother had tried, Emma hadn't been open to learning anything much from her. She wished she could turn back the clocks and listen to what she had to say.

While she and her grandfather leaned on each other by the graveside, Emma struggled to come to terms with the fact that within a couple of weeks her family of five had been reduced to two. She glanced at her grandfather, and saw that the lines on his face looked deeper and his hair somehow seemed more grey. She wondered how he would cope without her grandmother. They were so much in love, so devoted to one another. They'd been married for forty-six years, and as far as Emma knew, had spent no more than two weeks apart from each other in that entire time. Emma's heart ached as she recalled her grandmother's last message. What was it she was going to tell her? Would she ever find out now? Why didn't she listen to her messages sooner?

Soon after the final closing words of the service, the mourners gradually left, murmuring their condolences to Emma and her grandfather as they passed them. Not long later, it was just the two of them. They stood in silence, looking at the casket as it sat waiting to be lowered into the depths below. Emma was vaguely aware of a team of men waiting to finish the burial, but she ignored them for now.

"Granddad? Do you know what it was that Gran wanted to tell me the day before she died?"

He looked at her, tears staining his cheeks. "No, I'm afraid I don't."

"Oh, okay." Emma looked across the memorial garden and saw a bench in the distance, under a weeping willow. She took hold of her grandfather's hand.

"Let's go sit over there for a while."

She tugged gently, and her grandfather followed her with little resistance. Once settled on the bench, overlooking fields, facing away from where the men had already moved in to do their jobs, Emma smoothed out her black skirt and sighed.

A sound made her look up, and she realised that her grandfather had dissolved into sobs. Tears running down her own face, she lifted his arm and snuggled underneath it. As she looked at the fields through her blurry vision, the feeling of comfort and the view gave her a sudden sense of déjà vu. When a blue butterfly landed suddenly on her knee, her dream came rushing back to her in vivid detail. She realised that she had probably dreamed it after her grandmother had passed away. Was that her way of letting her know she was okay? Emma closed her eyes and tried to remember as much of the dream as possible. When she remembered the last words her grandmother said, she smiled. She watched the butterfly fly away and hugged her grandfather tighter.

"I had a dream last night, about Gran. We were sat on a bench just like this one in a park. She told me that everything would be okay, and that she loved you. She said that she loved you with all her heart and soul."

There was a deep silence, and she realised he had stopped crying. She looked up at his face and saw that her grandfather was smiling.

\* \* \*

Back in her flat once again, Emma stood in the window, watching the traffic and people below. The sorrow that had lifted a little, now returned with full force. She felt so empty. What else could possibly go wrong? Her life had been completely turned inside out, upside down then trampled on. She was an orphan with just one relative left.

She sighed. Perhaps she should go and stay with her grandfather for a while. She wished now that she had stayed with her grandparents after the first funeral. At least then she would have had more time with her grandmother before she died. She might have found out what she wanted to tell her, too. And the whole thing with Richard might never have happened. Her stomach clenched as she thought of him. He'd left another threatening message. She knew she should do something about it, but she just didn't have the energy to involve the police and make a complaint. Besides, how could she prove anything? She'd washed the sheets and thrown everything from that night away. The only thing she had was the messages on the machine. What could they do from that? Not much, probably.

Emma sighed again. She didn't want to be on her own tonight. And she figured that her grandfather probably didn't either. She nodded to herself, making the decision. She headed for her bedroom, grabbing a small suitcase from the hallway cupboard on her way.

Half an hour later, Emma stood at her front door. Considering the last message, she was slightly apprehensive about leaving her flat, and she hesitated as she unlocked the door. Taking a deep breath, she opened it and peered out, looking up and down the corridor. It was clear. Breathing a little easier, she stepped out with her suitcase and pulled the door shut behind her. Glancing over her shoulder, feeling slightly ridiculous, Emma made her way to the stairwell. She hoisted up the suitcase, grumbling to herself about her inability to pack light and made her way carefully down the stairs.

She set her suitcase down at the bottom, and pushed open the heavy fire door. She didn't even have time to scream before the hand clamped across her mouth and everything went dark.

* * *

Everything was black. Emma tried to open her eyes but found she couldn't. She tried to see why but then realised her hands were tied up. She tried to call out but found she was gagged. Her mind whirled in shock, trying to piece together what had happened, where she was, who had done this. She wriggled around, but found that she was completely incapacitated.

"There's not much point, bitch. You ain't going no-where."

The sound of Richard's voice made her heart jump into her throat and she gagged on the cloth in her mouth.

"Did you think I would let it go? Did you think I would let you get away with it?"

Emma smelt the alcohol on his breath as she tried to make sense of what he was saying.

"Where have you hidden it? What have you done with it?"

Emma gagged again when she realised what he was talking about. She couldn't answer him while gagged, but when he ungagged her, he was not going to like what she had to say. If he was capable of drugging her, raping her, knocking her out, gagging, blindfolding and tying her up, what else was he capable of doing? Was he going to kill her? She didn't think her grandfather would cope with having to attend yet another funeral.

She thought hard, trying to come up with an acceptable answer to his question. She could of course just keep denying that the wallet was in her flat, but then if he had planted it deliberately as she suspected, he would know she was lying.

As she had feared, a few moments later, he pulled the gag out of her mouth. She swallowed a couple of times, trying to wet her dry throat.

"So, where is it, bitch? Where have you hidden it?"

She heard drawers rattling and things being thrown to the ground and she realised then that she was in her own flat. She felt the surface she was laying on with her fingertips, and realised she was on the settee. She swallowed a few more times, and cleared her throat.

A rush of air alerted her a second before her head was roughly yanked back. She let out a squeal of pain as he almost pulled her hair out.

"Tell me now!" he snarled into her ear. Her body shaking, Emma tried to speak.

"I, I don't know, I don't-"

"You don't know? Don't lie to me!"

The alcohol fumes and the crazy tone of his voice made Emma go cold. She berated herself once more for not realising before how crazy he really was. Her hair still in his grip, she thought hard, but just couldn't come up with an acceptable answer. A feeling of resignation swept over her and she stopped shaking long enough to tell him the truth.

To her surprise, her hair was released, and she waited, listening to his ragged breathing.

"A kid stole the money and dumped the rest in the bin?" he asked, his voice incredulous.

"Yes."

Moments passed, and Emma tried to breathe normally. She had no idea what he was going to do next. But there was absolutely nothing she could do about it, either. She heard him move away, his footsteps soft on the lounge carpet. Then she heard his steps on the kitchen tiles. All sorts of wild ideas ran through her head. What was he doing? What was he looking for? She heard the scrape of the cutlery drawer, and her heart dropped. She knew what he was looking for, and by the sound of his returning footsteps, she knew he'd found it too.

*Oh God*, she thought. *Granddad, I am so sorry. I really don't want to leave you here by yourself. I'm so, so sorry. I love you.* Part of her was terrified, knowing that she would probably suffer a great deal of pain in the next few moments, but another part of her was calm, almost… happy. She would soon be with her parents and grandmother again. She missed them so much, and she hadn't really had time to properly grieve for them.

Well, now she wouldn't have to.

She could smell the alcohol as he leaned close to her face.

"Any last words, slut?"

Emma used every bit of willpower she had and remained silent. She refused to give him the pleasure of seeing her beg for mercy.

"Fine, I guess not."

Emma took a deep breath.

"Emma?!"

Shock slammed into her when she heard his voice. "Granddad!" she cried. "Don't come in here, he's crazy!" She didn't hear the fist sail toward her face, but she tasted the blood in her mouth when her tooth went through her lip.

"What the hell are you doing to my granddaughter?"

She'd never heard her grandfather sound so angry. Emma wriggled about, wishing she could see. "Granddad, don't! He has a knife!" She swallowed more blood and strained to listen.

"Well, now. This does complicate matters a little," Richard drawled. The crazy tone was back.

"Get away from my granddaughter."

"You mean this little slut? I've already had my way with her and let me tell you, she was crap. Which is what you would expect from a filthy little bitch like her. After all, just look at her fami-"

Emma heard her grandfather utter something before she heard a scuffle and Richard being cut off mid-sentence.

There was a struggle and Emma heard their feet dancing across the carpet. Then suddenly she heard a gasp, and then the sound of someone slumping to the floor. Heavy breathing followed. Emma stayed completely still, afraid to call out to find out what had happened. When she smelled the alcohol on the hot breath again, her lip trembled.

"Tell anyone who did this and you'll be next, bitch."

A few moments later he was gone, and Emma tried to calm down her breathing to listen for any other sounds. When she heard none, she started screaming.

# Chapter Fifteen

For hours, she was questioned by the police, but she refused to say anything. The terror of the ordeal had finally caught up with her, and she sat silently, clutching the blanket the paramedic had given her, twisting the fibres of the fabric with her fingers.

A neighbour had heard her screams and had come running. When the blindfold was removed, the scene before her was one that would be burned into her memory forever. Her eyes finally free, she began to sob when she saw the crumpled form of her grandfather on the floor. Her neighbour rushed over to him and tried to revive him, but Emma knew that it was too late. There was just too much blood.

"Emma? Can you hear me? We need to try and find out what happened, we need to know as much as possible to try and catch the person responsible for this. Do you understand?"

Emma did understand. She understood that if she said anything about the identity of the killer, she would be the next to die. Richard was crazy, and she didn't trust the police enough to take care of him before he took care of her.

She heard the two police officers whisper to each other,

and tuned them out. It really didn't matter anymore. In fact, did it even matter if Richard did kill her? What did she have left to live for anyway? Her entire family was gone. Wiped out. Dead. Why would she want to survive?

But then the memory of being gagged and bound, of his hot, alcoholic breath on her cheek came back to her and she faltered. She couldn't go through that again. She just couldn't. No, she wasn't afraid of dying, but she was afraid of how Richard would do it.

She remained silent.

Minutes later, a nurse entered the room and spoke to the police, telling them that Emma was in shock, and that it was likely that they wouldn't get any sense out of her that night. They left, leaving their card on the bedside table, asking her to call them if she remembered anything.

The nurse checked her vitals and asked her if there was anything she needed. Emma looked up at the nurse, a tear escaping down her cheek.

"I want my mum."

\* \* \*

After an overnight stay, Emma was discharged and found herself in front of the hospital, wondering where to go. A cab pulled up and without thinking, she jumped in and directed the cabbie to her flat.

The first thing she noticed when she stepped out onto the pavement was her grandfather's car, parked outside the café down the road. Her throat tightened and she wished that she hadn't called him yesterday to say she was coming to stay. If he hadn't known, he wouldn't have come looking for her when she didn't turn up. The second thing she noticed was the police cars. Fighting the tears, she entered the building and made her way up the stairs. When she reached her corridor, she slowed up, not wanting to have to speak to the police, but at the same time, wanting to get something from her flat before moving on.

The officer standing outside her door stopped her.

"Can I help you, Miss?"

Emma peered in and realised she didn't recognise any of the officers inside. She began speaking before the plan had completely formed in her mind. "Oh, I'm Rachael, a friend of Emma's who lives here. She's staying with me, but she wanted me to come and get some things for her."

The lies rolled off her tongue effortlessly, but her heart thudded when she saw him peer closely at her face.

"What happened to your lip, Rachael?"

Emma waved her hand. "Oh, nothing, my little brother loves to play baseball, I wasn't paying attention and the ball hit me in the face," Emma prattled on, praying he would believe her.

He did. With a shrug, he let her through, and then followed her in, explaining her presence to the other officers who were searching the flat for evidence.

"Just don't touch anything in the lounge, okay?"

"Oh, she wanted me to get the picture off the coffee table, is that alright?" Emma asked.

The officers glanced at each other, the one from the door shrugged again. "Sure, that's fine, but don't touch anything else."

Emma nodded and carefully picked her way through the lounge, avoiding the bloodstain on the carpet to get the framed picture of herself and her parents. She went into her bedroom and saw the suitcase she'd packed the day before. She looked around the room, wondering if there was anything else she wanted to take. Not that she could really take anything where she was planning to go. She really had only wanted the photograph, but she figured she should continue her charade to get past the police. She counted to a hundred then picked the suitcase up and left the bedroom. She waved to the officers.

"Thanks, think I've got everything. Bye." Her gaze locked on the answering machine in the corner of the room. She suddenly remembered that she never deleted the threatening messages from Richard. Maybe she didn't need to say anything after all. Once the police heard the messages, there would be no doubt that they would suspect him.

She left the flat, and said goodbye to the officer outside. She headed for the stairs again, feeling a sense of déjà vu. Her life seemed to be going round in circles lately, and she decided that it was time to break the cycle. She emerged from the building, and rummaged in her pocket for the keys that she had been given at the hospital, along with her grandfather's watch and other belongings. She went to his car, threw the suitcase in the boot, jumped in, and without a backward glance, drove away.

\* \* \*

The silence of the house was overwhelming. While Emma wandered from room to room, touching things, looking at photographs, the memories of her childhood flooded back. She ended up in her grandparents' bedroom and sat on their neatly made bed. She wondered what would happen to the house, to her parents' house. She didn't care what happened to her flat. After being so pleased with it in the beginning, she never wanted to see it again.

She traced the outline of her grandparents' faces in the framed photograph next to the bed. They looked so incredibly happy. As a child she'd loved to sit and listen to her grandmother's stories. No matter what was going on, her grandmother always had a story to tell. Her gaze caught a neat stack of books on the bedside table, bearing her grandmother's name. It was too late to read her words now.

She tried to recall the story of when her grandparents had first met, but her memory was hazy. She wished she had asked her grandfather about the mention of meeting in their dreams first. It had seemed like a magical tale when she was a child, but after her dream about her grandmother in the park, she now wondered about the truth of it.

As she stood up to leave, Emma's gaze was caught by a glint of metal on her grandmother's dresser. She went over to find her watch. Emma picked it up and slid it on her wrist. It fit perfectly. Her grandmother had always worn it, even though as far as she could remember, it had never worked. She'd said that it had been her grandmother's. Emma caught sight of herself in the mirror. Her grandmother had always said she looked just like her own grandmother had when she was younger. Right now, all Emma could see were red puffy eyes, frown lines, a swollen lip and sheer exhaustion.

Turning away from her reflection, she turned to look at the photo on the bedside table. "Goodbye, Gran, Granddad. I love you. Hopefully I'll see you soon."

\* \* \*

Emma sat in the car outside her parents' house. She had planned to go inside, to be in her childhood home once more, but she didn't think she had the strength to. If she was going to follow through with her final plan, she needed to do it as quickly as possible, before her common sense kicked in and she changed her mind.

Looking away from the house, Emma turned the key in the ignition and started the car. Calm now, and certain of her decision, she drove carefully through the village she had once run around as a child. Past the homes of old friends, the school, park and out into the countryside. When she reached the main rural road, she drove a little faster, enjoying the feeling of speed as she whipped around the tight corners, the trees rushing past in a green blur. After a couple of near misses however, she slowed slightly. She had no intention of anyone else getting hurt today.

Not really sure of where she was headed for, Emma kept driving, looking for a suitable place. Finally, signs for a woodland path came into sight up ahead, and Emma took the first turning off into the forest. She drove for a few miles, then stopped in a clearing. Satisfied that she wouldn't be heard here, nor indeed found too quickly afterwards, Emma stopped the car, switched off the engine and got out. She walked to the boot of the car and opened it. She opened the heavy metal case and pulled out the gun. It was very heavy, and very old. It had been her grandfather's when he was a young boy, back when ordinary people were allowed to own guns. She'd never used one herself, but she'd seen enough old films with her grandfather to understand how they worked.

She loaded the gun, and was just taking off the safety when a noise behind her startled her. She spun around, keeping the gun out of sight, and her eyes widened.

On the other side of the clearing, where only moments before there had been just trees, sat a large log cabin. Emma blinked several times, unable to believe her eyes. She squinted at the sign hung above the doorway.

'Pam's Tearooms.'

She shook her head in amazement. How hadn't she noticed it when she pulled up? She looked at the windows, trying to see if there was anyone inside. She didn't see any movement, but that didn't mean there wasn't anyone out the back. She turned back to the car, looking down at the gun. Well, there was no way she could do this here. She set the gun back in the box and closed it. She closed the boot and went to the driver's side door, fully intending to get in the car and find somewhere more suitable, but something stopped her. A sudden overwhelming need for a strong cup of tea overtook her, and she locked the door instead. Frowning at her own actions, she walked slowly over toward the log cabin.

# Chapter Sixteen

"Gran?"

"Evelyn?"

The two women stood, staring at one another in disbelief. Natalie peered closer and realised that the wreck of a girl in front of her wasn't Evelyn at all, but she bore a striking resemblance to the woman who had left the tearooms in all her fifties glory. This girl was a much sorrier state, and looked just as confused as Natalie felt.

The girl came closer, then frowned. "I'm sorry, for a minute there, you looked like my grandmother."

Natalie smiled, snapping herself out of her own shock. "That's okay, sweetheart, why don't you come in and join me for a nice cup of tea?"

The girl looked a little hesitant, but finally went over to the nearest table and sat down. Natalie went to the kitchen and got a fresh pot of tea, along with some cherry and coconut cake, feeling a familiar sense of déjà vu as she did. Though she knew the girl wasn't Evelyn, from what she was sensing from her energy, she also knew that the conversation she was about to have would probably be very similar to the same one she'd had in this very same place, so many years before.

She set the cups and plates on the table, noting more similarities in the girl's face and mannerisms. There was no doubt in her mind. This girl was a relative of hers, which meant that the time had finally come.

Natalie poured the tea, and took a sip, waiting for the girl to begin her story. Though she knew that she had come to take over, and that Natalie would soon be showing her how to run Pam's, she had no idea what the girl's story would be, or what had brought her to this place. She held back from reading her energy or her aura too much, because part of her was afraid to know.

The silence stretched on, and Natalie realised that the girl hadn't touched her cake.

"Please, sweetheart, go ahead. I made it fresh this morning."

The girl nodded and took a tiny bite of the cake. She swallowed and nodded. "It's good."

"So, why don't you tell me what's wrong?" Natalie asked gently.

The girl looked up at her, sadness, weariness, fear and sorrow etched in her face. With a defeated sigh, she began the story, starting with the awful day that her parents had died.

\* \* \*

Natalie wished she hadn't asked.

Though the girl, whose name was Emma, hadn't elaborated too much with the details, Natalie now knew that her whole family had died within the space of a few weeks. If this girl was indeed her granddaughter, which, according to the current date on earth would fit – that meant that Natalie's own daughter and son-in-law were going to be killed in a car accident, she herself was going to die in her sleep, and her husband was going to die in an awful attack. Natalie struggled to keep her composure, wondering how Evelyn had managed to keep hers all those years ago when Natalie had told her the demise of her family.

Natalie's heart went out to the young girl, her grand-daughter, who was now in very similar circumstances to Natalie herself when she'd entered the dimension. Except that Natalie hadn't had a deranged psycho who wanted to murder her, just a broken heart.

When the girl had finished her story, the tea was going cold, the cake was merely crumbs on their plates. Natalie wondered how to approach the subject of how Emma was here to take over an alternate dimension and help people who had reached the end of their tether. She decided to copy Evelyn's approach, and hoped that Emma would find it easier to understand than she had.

"Tell me, Emma, what did you come to this world to do?"

Emma frowned at her. "What do you mean?"

"What is your mission in life? What do you want to accomplish?"

Emma sighed. She pushed the crumbs around her plate with her fork for a few seconds then dropped the fork with a clatter. She looked up at Natalie and shrugged.

"I don't know. I don't have a purpose anymore. I just know that I don't want to live anymore. I just don't see the point."

Natalie swallowed hard at Emma's words. She looked so beaten, so lost. Natalie couldn't stand it anymore. She stood up and went over to her. She put her arms around her and Emma let her pull her close.

"I'm here, sweetheart. I'm here." Natalie said, hugging

her close. She felt Emma shake as she began to cry.

* * *

It had taken numerous cups of tea before Natalie had finally gathered the courage to tell Emma the truth. She left out the part that she was indeed her grandmother, not wanting Emma to become distracted from the complicated matter at hand.

She tried her best to explain, and they were now stood in the supermarket, as Emma tried to comprehend what she was being shown. She was picking it all up remarkably quickly, but Natalie felt that Emma was so exhausted, it probably wasn't making much sense.

She decided to take her to the park, so they could rest and Emma could ask her more questions.

When they arrived on the bench, Emma let out a gasp as she looked around. She turned to stare at Natalie, a smile lighting up her face.

"I understand now."

Natalie's eyebrows shot up. "You do?" She glanced around the park, wondering what had made everything so clear.

"This is like heaven, isn't it? It's a dimension people go to when they die?"

Natalie was surprised. "Well, yes, sometimes they do come here when they die, but mainly the people we help here are still alive. They are at the darkest point of their existence and are in need of help to pick themselves back up."

Emma nodded, smiling. For the first time since she walked through the door of the tearoom, she looked relaxed.

Natalie patted Emma's hand and noticed for the first

time the watch on her wrist. She was sure it was Evelyn's.

Emma saw her looking at it and held it up for her to see better. "This was my grandmother's watch. It's never worked, but she wore it every day anyway." Emma smiled. "She was never late for anything, so it must have made sense to her somehow."

Natalie bit her lip as she remembered Evelyn and wondered if she should tell Emma the truth, that she was really her grandmother, but seeing as Evelyn hadn't told her, she held back.

"Do you have any other questions?"

Emma shook her head. "This is what my grandmother wanted to tell me. I'm sure of it. It all kind of makes sense now, in a weird way."

"Really?"

"Yes, the night she passed away, I dreamed about her, and we were sat on a bench, in a park. This bench. This park. I think she wanted me to come here."

Natalie was amazed. She hadn't expected Emma to understand everything so quickly. She hadn't expected that she herself would be leaving the dimension so quickly. She wondered if she was ready. But then, Emma wouldn't have turned up if she wasn't.

They sat for a while longer, and Natalie gave Emma her notebook.

"I hope this will help you. There have been a great many changes here in the last fifty years, and I am sure there will be many more to come. But somehow, I'm sure that you will be able to keep up with them better than I did."

Emma flicked through some of the pages, reading a sentence here and there in Natalie's neat, flowing script. She closed it and held it to her chest.

"Thank you. I'm sure it will be useful. Gran wrote several

books, I wish now that I had read them."

"Check out Pam's Bookstore, they have every book in existence, not to mention every book that might exist."

"Seriously? I will, thank you."

Feeling no need to delay the inevitable any longer, Natalie took them back to the tearooms. Just to give herself a little more time to prepare, Natalie made them some tea. They had just sat down to drink it when Natalie sensed someone arriving. She recognised the energy and frowned. It was unlike William to come when she was with someone, but then maybe he had sensed she would be leaving soon. Though he should have known she wouldn't leave without saying goodbye to him first. She looked up as he walked in and she caught his eye and motioned to Emma, in a signal for him to leave. To her surprise, he shook his head and smiled. He continued walking over to them, and stopped by their table.

"What's this? No cake?"

Emma looked up, startled at his sudden arrival and her eyes widened. "Granddad?"

William smiled at her and nodded. She threw herself into his arms as Natalie watched, amazed.

"What are you doing here?" Emma cried, holding onto him tightly, afraid to let him go.

"I just had a few things to take care of, before moving on."

"I'm so sorry, Granddad. I'm so sorry for what happened. I didn't know he was like that, I swear."

"Shhh, it's okay, sweetie pie. It's okay. I know you didn't. I'm just so pleased that you found your way here."

"You knew about this place before?"

"Yes, this is where I met your grandmother."

Emma pulled away then, and looked at her grandfather.

Then she turned to look at Natalie, who was sat with her mouth wide open.

"Are you saying...?"

"Yes," Natalie chimed in. "Are you saying that you're my husband?"

William smiled at Natalie. "Yes, I am." He looked at Emma. "And yes, that is your grandmother."

Emma's eyes widened again and she rushed over to Natalie, throwing herself into her lap. Natalie hugged her tightly, overcome with emotion from the display of love from her granddaughter.

William watched them both, a smile on his face.

"Shall I get us some more tea? How about some cake this time?"

* * *

"There's one thing that's been bothering me."

Natalie looked at her granddaughter and nodded encouragingly. "Yes? What is it?"

Emma paused for a few moments, as though unsure of how to say it. "Why didn't you tell me about this dimension sooner? Why did you let me lose my parents and lose you and granddad? I mean, after my parents died, you asked me to come and stay with you, but I said no. If you had made me, then maybe the thing with Richard wouldn't have happened, and Granddad would still be alive."

Natalie looked to William for support. He put his hand on hers and squeezed it.

"Oh, sweetheart," Natalie said. "I wish more than anything that there was some way I could have prevented you from going through such an awful time, but the truth is, if you hadn't been through so much, you might not have found your way to me here, now."

"You don't know that. I might have. You said earlier that more souls were finding Pam's, even when they weren't at their lowest point."

"That's true. In all honesty, I don't know what to say. I can only apologise."

"Sweetie, you don't have to feel guilty about what happened to me," William added. "It wasn't your fault. Besides, it's just so good to be back here again, to see your grandmother again."

Emma nodded. "I understand, I guess. I suppose it will just take a little time to get over it all."

"Time is something you will find plenty of here." Natalie smiled.

"I guess the only other thing I don't understand is why you look different here, to when you are in the earthly dimension."

Natalie nodded. "I thought the same when I met my grandmother here. She looked so different, that I didn't even realise she was my grandmother! I only found out after she left. In this dimension, I can change my appearance at will, as you will be able to. And so time only has an effect on my appearance because I expect it to. Even then, I can control how I age, and what I look like, whereas on earth, we don't have that kind of control…" she broke off and frowned. She could feel an unfamiliar tugging at the edge of her consciousness. Her eyes were drawn to the door, and she thought she saw a glimmer of light around the edges.

William noticed her silence and placed his hand over hers.

"Is it time?"

She looked at him and nodded. She took a shallow breath, suddenly overcome with what was about to happen.

Emma smiled at her, looking like a completely different person to the girl who had walked through the door not long before.

"It's okay, Gran, if you need to go, then you should. I'll be fine here."

William smiled. "I can always stay a while to help if you want."

Emma nodded. "I'd like that."

Natalie looked from her husband and grandchild, whom in her own reality she had yet to meet or produce, and smiled too.

"I love you both, so much. Don't ever forget that."

They both nodded, and as one they rose from the table. Slowly, holding hands, the three of them walked to the door.

Natalie hugged Emma, and kissed her on the cheek. "Though I know you won't need it, good luck, sweetheart."

"Thank you, Gran, I love you." A tear slid down Emma's cheek and Natalie smoothed it away.

Remembering the handkerchief in her pocket, she took it out and handed it to Emma.

Emma saw the initials and smiled. "These are my initials."

"They were my grandmother's initials, too." Natalie smiled, her eyes welling up as she squeezed her granddaughter's hand for the last time. She turned to William.

"Why didn't you tell me that I was your wife? I would never have sent you away if I had known."

"I know, but I didn't know until this moment if you were supposed to know. Also, I was spending so much time with you while I was awake, I needed a break while I was sleeping."

Natalie punched him lightly on the arm. "Hey, stop

joking about."

William chuckled. "I'm sorry. I didn't mean it. But do you know the best thing?"

"No, what?"

"All the times we've had together, all the years we have spent in each other's company, are all yet to come for you. You get to experience them all now, and I get to experience them with you."

Natalie smiled. "You're right." She glanced at the door. "I guess I'd better get going then."

William nodded. "Yes, you should." He reached out and pulled her to him, kissing her gently on the lips. Surprised, but glad that they were finally having their first kiss, she pressed herself closer, deepening the kiss. If her granddaughter hadn't been standing right behind her, she would have kissed him longer, but reluctantly, she pulled away. Before she stepped away, he leaned down to whisper in her ear.

"I love you, Jemima. I love you with all my heart and soul."

She looked up at him, surprised. "How did you know my middle name?"

William shook his head and rolled his eyes. "I was married to you, I know everything there is to know about you. Besides, when I met you on earth that was the name you were using."

"It was? Interesting." Natalie sighed, the tugging was getting more insistent. "I have to go."

William nodded and stepped back. Emma joined him and he put his arm around her.

Natalie smiled at them both. "I guess I'll see you both again soon then."

She took a deep breath and a strange feeling washed

over her. When she looked down, she was dressed in the same clothing as when she'd arrived in the tearoom and met Evelyn. She looked up at William and Emma one last time and smiled. She finally felt ready to return. She took another deep breath and turned to walk through the door, into the glimmering light.

# Chapter Seventeen

Natalie blinked, her eyes adjusting from the bright light to the darkness of the clearing in the woods. She glanced behind her to see nothing but the shadows of trees. She peered into the darkness and saw her car, still sat where she had rolled to a stop, fifty years before. She walked toward it and was surprised to notice that the engine sounded like it was still cooling. She laid a hand on the bonnet. It was warm.

Though she had tried many times to imagine what this moment would feel like, nothing had really prepared her for going back in time in this way. She realised she was holding her handbag, and pulled out her keys. She unlocked the car and got in. Briefly she wondered what she would do if after all this time, she had forgotten how to drive, but it all came naturally to her. She started the car and pulled away, heading for the main road.

When she reached her flat, she remembered the film she had watched of herself, when she had returned to her life. She did exactly what she had in the film, clearing out all reminders of Phillip. She felt no need for them now, after all her time at Pam's, she had got over him completely. She felt nothing but a fondness for him now. If it wasn't for his rejection, she would never have found Pam's in the first place. She recalled the paragraph she had read from the book she would write one day and found the photo of Evelyn in her memory box. Though she hadn't mentioned it in her book, she also found Evelyn's watch. She recalled what Emma had said, and so wasn't surprised to see that it didn't work. She slid it on her wrist anyway, feeling closer to both Evelyn and Emma as she did so. She knew that every time she looked at it, she would remember them and remember her time at Pam's.

Time passed quickly and she changed many things, turning her life around. One of the first things she did was to start using her second name. She didn't know if it was because of what William had said, or if it was because it felt like the right thing to do. Either way, she was determined to make a new start. A new life, a new name, a new perspective. And, she decided, it was time for a new location. With excitement, she packed up her belongings and moved a few hours away, to the village where Emma's parents and grandparents had lived.

When she arrived there, she threw herself into the community, getting involved in local events and getting herself a job in the local bookstore. After being in Pam's Bookstore so often, she felt very much at home selling books, and helping people find the one they needed. Occasionally, she even found herself able to see people's auras, though she couldn't read them like she could in the other dimension.

* * *

A couple of years later, she was putting away a new shipment of books, and she found herself in the Mind Body Spirit section. She found a book on Energy Healing and was flipping through it when someone bumped into her, making her drop it.

"Oh, I'm sorry! I didn't see you there."

Unable to believe her ears, she looked up at the man.

"William?" she whispered.

He took a step back, shocked. "How did you know that? I never use my first name anymore." He frowned, and looked at her more closely. "Have we met before? In the supermarket, maybe?"

Jemima blinked. The memory of their meeting in the supermarket came back to her and she smiled.

"Yes, I think we have met before." She held her hand out. "My name's Jemima."

"Nice to meet you properly, Jemima. My name is James by the way. But you can call me William if you want."

Jemima smiled. She bent down to pick up the forgotten book at her feet. She re-shelved it and looked at William, a cheeky smile on her face.

"Anything I can help you find today? 'The Beginner's Guide to the Kama Sutra', perhaps?"

# Evelyn's Famous
# Cherry and Coconut Cake

## Ingredients:

5oz Sugar
5oz Butter
3 Eggs
8oz Flour
2oz Desiccated Coconut
3oz Chopped Glace Cherries

## Method:

Cream the butter and sugar together, then add the eggs.
Stir in the flour, coconut and cherries.
Put the mixture in a lined or greased loaf tin, and bake at
180°C for 45 mins to an hour.

# Natalie's Family Tree

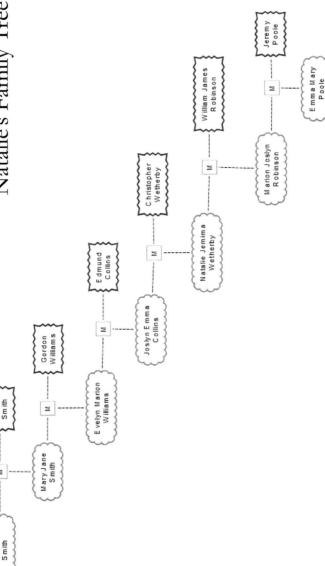

*Bonus Book:*

# Choose Your Own Reality

By

Michelle Gordon

theamethystangel.com

First published in Great Britain in 2011 by The Amethyst Angel
Second Edition Published in Great Britain in 2014 by The Amethyst Angel

The suggestions in this book are not to be substituted for medical or professional attention. Any application of this method is at the reader's sole discretion and risk. The author and the publisher accept no responsibility for the consequences of using the information given in the book.

Second Edition.

# Introduction

When I was younger, a child of the eighties and nineties, before the advent of computer games, I loved the 'Choose Your Own Adventure' books. The idea of being able to control the way the story ended, was enticing to me. Although I must admit, more often than not, I would cheat and check to see which ending was best. I didn't like 'dying' too quickly as it meant there was less book to read! Now, with millions of different computer games, each with a seemingly unlimited number of outcomes, it seems quite normal to us to be able to control the destiny of the animated character on the screen. So why shouldn't it be the same for ourselves?

Recent years have seen a massive increase in books, DVDs, CDs etc. that show us, in one way or another, how to create our own lives, how to order things we want from the Universe and how to change our lives for the better. Some of these books have undoubtedly worked for many, and yet people continue to buy more books, more CDs and more DVDs. Each with their own interpretations, theories and ideas on how life works, how we can get what we want and how we can live a life full of meaning and purpose.

I'm not going to profess to have found the ultimate

answer, or the one and only way, because I believe that there are more answers than there are questions, and that there are more ways of living life than there are people. But this book is about the way that I have found works for me and for others I have shared it with. If you find it works for you as well, then use it, play with it, modify it – there are no rules! If you find that it doesn't work for you, then I wish you all the best in finding the way that does.

Life has become a whole lot more complicated in the last few decades. We have graduated from those simple adventure books to being able to read any one of millions of books on a tiny portable screen at the click of a button. We have gone from a few choices to more than we can imagine. When it comes to the spiritual and self-help industry, it's no different. There are meditations, spells, magic formulas, special words, sacred spaces, tools etc. All of which have worked for people, all of which have their place in this amazingly diverse world that we live in. But personally, I prefer to keep things simple. My life is complicated enough without needing to buy any special ingredients to make things work the way I want them to. So before we get to the point, let's move on to where it began for me.

# How it all began

My memory is not the best, but the beginning of this journey still remains quite clear to me. I was living on my own in the East Midlands in England. Though I had begun my spiritual journey a few years before, things were still going in fits and starts. I read everything I could get my hands on, and my favourite authors included Neale Donald Walsch, Doreen Virtue, Eckhart Tolle and Louise L. Hay, to name just a few. But still, my life wasn't going quite the way I wished it would. One night, while watching an excellent movie called Déja Vu, I had a moment of clarity which prompted me to not only have a conversation with God, but also to have some realisations on the way things might work.

As all of my favourite authors have pointed out, time as we know it does not exist. We see it as being linear, from past flowing into the future. But how is it then that some people are able to see into the future and predict what's going to happen? Why are there so many theories and stories which include the ability to time-travel, visiting the past or the future? How does that fit into the theory that the past is merely a memory and the future is just an idea?

I know that you may well have read many books already

that discuss theories of time, and therefore I won't go into great detail, because as you know, I like to keep things simple. So I want you to imagine for a moment that there are in fact alternate realities. That while you are reading this book in this reality, there are a multitude of realities in which you are doing something else entirely. Then I want you to imagine that all of those realities, and all of your past and future realities all exist in this very moment. That they are all happening at the same time. In this moment. Right now. Can you imagine that? After all, in another reality, this book may well have never been published, and therefore you would be reading something else, or even doing something else.

If you can imagine this, if you can see every imaginable reality existing in a single dot, an eternal circle, then is it so difficult to believe that we can choose which reality we want to experience? Is it difficult to believe that you have in fact chosen to experience your current reality? It may not have been a conscious choice, but I assure you, you most definitely chose it yourself. So what does this mean? Well, it means that we don't experience anything that we don't choose. Again, this is something that has been said before, and so it is no great revelation. But what I realised, in my moment of clarity, is that unlike the teachings of some books, that say we create our own lives, we create our own realities, that we create with our thoughts; this is something far simpler.

I don't know about you, but I find the process of creation to be quite a tough one. I'm quite creative in the sense that I love to make things. I sew, I knit, I make notebooks, teddy bears, rugs – you name a craft and I've probably tried it. I just love to make something out of raw materials. But I also find it quite daunting at times. Sometimes, I even put off making something entirely because I feel I can't devote enough time to it, or I can't quite do it justice. And always, without fail, when I decide to make something, the end product never looks like the original picture I had in my head. Sometimes it's better, but most of the time, it's just completely different. So when it comes to creating my own life, my own reality, to me, it just seems far too daunting. Not to mention a lot of hard work. What a relief it was to realise then, that if every possible reality exists right now, surely I could just choose which one I wanted? After all, how can you create something when it already exists?

So I abandoned creation (well, when it came to my life anyway, the crafts still continued!) and threw myself into the art of choosing. Of course, like most people suggest, I decided to start out small. The more mini-successes I had, the more adventurous I got. And the more I believed in it, the more it worked. I shared the method with a few people and they found it worked too. Now, I want to share it with you, in the hopes that it will also help you to be able to experience the reality of your choosing.

# The Method

L ike all the best things in life, the method is really very simple, and consists of a few words. Whether these words are spoken, written or thought, they are powerful words, made all the more powerful by the intentions behind them. Are you ready? Here we go:

**I choose to tune into the reality where...**

Begin your sentences with this, and your life may never be the same again. Imagine that these simple words are the key to entering one of those alternate realities. Stating your desires in this way tells the Universe that you are ready to experience the reality that you choose. That you don't want to fool around, tinker with different ideas in order to try and create your life, but that this is what you want. Full stop.

The best way I can think to explain it is this – You need a new pair of shoes. Now, to get the pair that is exactly right for you, you could make them. You could choose the fabric, the style, take a shoe-making course, and then toil for hours, weeks or months to create the perfect pair of shoes. Or, alternatively, you could go into the right shop and choose the perfect pair of shoes and wear them immediately. Which would you prefer to do? As much as I like to be creative, I would much rather choose than create. Because if you can imagine it, if you can conceive it, then you can choose it. Because it must already exist if it exists in your mind.

So, how to use the method? Quite simply, you choose to experience whatever you desire using those words. I prefer to write these choices down, because I find it fascinating to look back and see which ones have happened. Let's take an example. Say you want a car. You could say:

"I choose to tune into the reality where I have a car."

Now, that would be perfectly fine, as long as you don't mind what car it is, what condition it's in or how it runs. Though this method is simple, being specific is quite important. Therefore, it would be better to word it thus:

"I choose to tune into the reality where I own a VW Beetle that's in excellent condition and runs well."

Of course, you could always choose the colour etc. too, but I like to have some surprises in my life, don't you?

Now of course, you may be thinking, if everything exists in this moment, then that VW Beetle should instantly appear the moment I make the request. Alas, it doesn't work that way. Mainly, because we don't believe it does. If a VW Beetle were to drop out of the sky and land right in front of you right now, you'd probably just have a heart attack and die, which wouldn't be a great idea. No, what is more likely to happen once the choice has been made, (and you do only need to state the choice once) is that the Universe will bring to you all sorts of opportunities for you to own a VW Beetle. Whether it's bringing your attention to an ad in the paper, or crossing your path with someone who owns one and is looking to sell it. You just need to be open to those opportunities, and follow your instincts and intuition. Also, you need to be open to alternatives. The Universe may not comply to your specifics, but it may bring something slightly different, and in most cases, better. So rather than holding on for your exact request, go with the flow, you never know where it might take you.

# What do you want?

The method is simple. By using just a few words at the beginning of your sentence, you have made your desires clear to the Universe, and you can rest assured that you will indeed experience them. What might not be so simple, however, is figuring out exactly what it is you want. The small things should be fairly straightforward, for example, you might be running a little late, and therefore need to find a good parking space close to your meeting. Or you've seen something you want to buy, but haven't got the funds to buy it at the moment. But the bigger, more life-altering choices? They might not be so easy. Though I'll tell you this – the clearer you are in your choices, the quicker and easier those realities come into your experience.

I think the biggest obstacle in choosing the reality we wish to experience is our tendency to wonder how it will happen. How. Such a small word, and yet such a debilitating one. When we want something, but we cannot figure out how it will happen, inevitably, we will believe it is not possible. Or at least, not possible for us. And then we discard that dream, that desire, that want, and move onto another one. But every now and then, we look back and wonder – what if? I don't know about you but I'd really rather not live a life of regret. So forget about how. How something is going to happen really isn't in your hands. That's up to the Universe. What you have to get absolutely clear on is WHAT. What do you really want? What does your heart desire? Only you can answer that. When you know, state that desire to the Universe and let it figure out how to make it possible.

# Tried and Tested

Well, that's it. Short, sweet and simple. But in case you're still shaking your head and saying it couldn't possibly be that simple, here's a few real-life examples.

When I first constructed this sentence-opener, I had absolute faith that it would work, but still needed some proof, so I set about using it on small things to begin with.

I'm not a morning person. Ask anyone who knows me, and they'll confirm this. When I lived in the East Midlands I had a job across town that required two bus journeys to get to. The first bus would depart from a stop ten minutes' walk away at 7.47am. Now, it didn't matter how early I got up, for the first few months of the job, I found myself late every time. And each time I arrived at the bus stop, sweaty and breathless from sprinting the last hundred yards, I would promise myself I'd get up earlier, leave the house earlier, etc. etc., but I never did. On the days I missed the bus, I would sit at the bus stop, muttering profanities at the unfairness of it all – how dare the bus driver leave two whole minutes early? It was a disgrace. Needless to say, I always arrived at work in a bad mood.

After my revelation of alternate realities and life ultimately being of our own choosing, I decided to simply choose to

~ 11 ~

'tune into' the reality where I caught the bus in the morning. The first few times I tried it, I thought it sheer luck. But as time wore on and I caught the bus every day, I began to wonder. Because I hadn't been getting up any earlier. In fact, most days I was getting up later than ever. And not only was I getting up later, but I was doing more in the morning. Before, I barely had time to brush my teeth, get dressed and scoff some cereal. After a few weeks of choosing my reality, I was not only having a lie-in, but I was cooking pancakes, checking my e-mail, and still managing to catch the 7.47am. How was this possible? Time itself seemed to be slowing down, all because I was tuning into a reality where I always caught the bus.

My confidence in my little sentence-opener started me off on a new journey, one where it truly seemed like anything were possible. It was only a matter of time before I used it to change my life completely.

In March 2008, I found myself with a plane ticket to California. It was originally booked for a wedding that was cancelled at the last minute. But I was not going to let the ticket go to waste, so I decided to go by myself. I had no itinerary, all I knew was that I was flying into San Francisco, and two weeks later, flying out of LA. I booked the first three nights in San Francisco in a hostel, but after that, who knew? It was one of the best things I have ever done. It was a holiday of magical serendipity, and the people I met and places I went will stay with me forever. But the one thing that really stood out for me, really struck me, and the reason I fell in love with LA, was the feeling of possibility. Everyone I met in LA had a dream. And not only did they have a dream, but they were pursuing it, actively. They knew exactly what they wanted, and would stop at nothing to get it. It made me look at my own life, and I realised that there was something that I really wanted. I wanted to live in America. This is something that I had wanted most of my life. I can't really explain it properly, but whenever I'm in America, I'm home.

I had been trying for four years by that point to find a way to move there but to no avail. I had started two university degrees, and quit both. I had started businesses, I had searched for jobs with prospects of transferring. But nothing was working. Just before my trip to California, I had pretty much given up on the idea. I didn't realise it then, but I see now that I was absolutely focused on the 'how'. How was I going to move there? How could I get a visa? How could I afford to live there? Because of that, I was closing myself off to opportunities that could make it work.

My two weeks in America were over far too quickly, and I suddenly went from sitting in the warm sunshine with a cute German pilot, eating waffles, to dragging my suitcase through London in the -3°C freezing rain. I remember this moment so clearly – I did not want to be in the UK. I didn't want to waste another moment. That night, I got home and I wrote in my travel diary:

"I choose to tune into the reality where I live in America by the end of this year."

I didn't even think about how it could possibly happen. I just knew, that I would be there. Two and a half months later, I was back in London, this time, boarding a plane to New York, and beginning a ten month adventure as an Au Pair.

Of course, not every instance where I have used this method has worked out well. In New York, the train ticket system works quite differently to the UK. There, you buy a ticket, then the conductor on-board punches it. If they don't, then it's still valid, and you could use it for another journey. While living in Westchester County, I made trips into the city quite often, so I bought a ten-trip ticket. One day, I was trying to get home by a certain time, and managed to catch the train seconds before it left Harlem station. I remember standing on the train, watching the super-slow progress of the conductor and hoping I would get away without having my ticket punched, so I could get an extra trip out of it. To make my wish clearer, I said to myself:

"I choose to tune into the reality where the conductor doesn't punch my ticket for this journey."

With only a few minutes to go before the train approached my stop, the conductor reached me and my heart sank. He took my ticket, looked down at it and said:

"You didn't want to go to New Rochelle did you?"

Confused, I nodded and he gave me a sympathetic smile.

"Well, I'm afraid this is the express train. It's not stopping until we reach Stamford, Connecticut."

He handed me the ticket back and I frantically made phone calls to sort out the appointment I would be very late for. It wasn't until I was on the train home from Stamford that I looked at my ticket and realised he hadn't punched it. So in fact, I did experience the reality I chose, but I didn't realise that the reality would take me on an unplanned trip to Connecticut, cost me extra money and make me very late for my appointment. I guess the old adage is true – Be careful what you wish for!

During my time in New York, I made some life-long friends, one of whom was very interested in my method of choosing my reality. She gave it a go, and although I had experienced success myself, I was amazed by the realities she was able to choose.

Somehow, she had managed to run up a very expensive cell phone bill, which went into hundreds of dollars. Being a nanny, she couldn't really afford the bill, and she was stressing over how on earth she would be able to pay it. I suggested she choose to tune into a reality where the bill was reduced, or where she found a way to pay it. So she wrote:

"I choose to tune into the reality where I pay only $100 for my cell phone bill."

Just a few days later, she received a call from the company, saying that because she'd been such a loyal customer for so long, they would reduce the massive bill. She paid just $98. And has been using the method ever since!

# Over to you

So there you have it. I promised this would be short, didn't I? If any of this book has resonated with you, then please, give this method a try. Modify it if you want, tell your friends about it, but most of all, have fun with it. If nothing in this book has resonated with you, then first of all, well done for making it this far, and second of all, why not give it a try anyway? You have nothing to lose!

One last thing: this book itself is the product of those simple words. When I first visited my boyfriend's house, I saw the balcony and thought to myself:

"I choose to tune into the reality where I sit on that balcony and write a book in the sunshine."

Well, I hope you've enjoyed reading it as much as I enjoyed sitting in the sun writing it.

# About the Author

Michelle lives in the UK, when she's not flitting in and out of other realms. She believes in Faeries and Unicorns and thinks the world needs more magic and fun in it. She writes because she would go crazy if she didn't. She might already be a little crazy, so please buy more books so she can keep writing.

Please feel free to write a review of this book. Michelle loves to get direct feedback, so if you would like to contact her, please e-mail theamethystangel@hotmail.co.uk or keep up to date by following her blog – **TwinFlameBlog.com.** You can also follow her on Twitter **@themiraclemuse** or like her page on Facebook.

You can now become an Earth Angel Trainee:
**earthangelacademy.co.uk**

To sign up to her mailing list, visit:
**michellegordon.co.uk**

# Where's My F**king Unicorn?

Are your bookshelves filled with self-help books, and yet your life feels empty? Do you keep following paths to enlightenment that lead to the same dead ends? You've read the books, attended the seminars and taken heed of every bit of advice going... but you're still waiting for your f**king unicorn to come along! Where's My F**king Unicorn? is a guide to life, creativity and happiness that offers a very different way forward. Author, Michelle Gordon, explains why, in spite of all your best efforts, your life still doesn't live up to your vision of what it should be, and tells you exactly what you can do about it. In refreshingly down-to-earth language, she shows you how to harness all the self-knowledge you have gained from all those self-help books you've read, and actually start putting it to practical use.

# Earth Angel Series:

## *The Earth Angel Training Academy (book 1)*

There are humans on Earth, who are not, in fact, human.

They are **Earth Angels**.

Earth Angels are beings who have come from other realms, dimensions and planets, and are choosing to be born on Earth in human form for just **one** reason.

To **Awaken the world**.

Before they can carry out their perilous mission, they must first learn how to be human.

The best place they can do that, is at

## **The Earth Angel Training Academy**

## *The Earth Angel Awakening (book 2)*

After learning how to be human at the Earth Angel Training Academy, the Angels, Faeries, Merpeople and Starpeople are born into human bodies on Earth.

Their Mission? **Awaken the world**.

But even though they **chose** to go to Earth, and they chose to be human, it doesn't mean that it will be **easy** for them to Awaken themselves.

Only if they **reconnect** to their **origins**, and to other Earth Angels, will they will be able to **remember** who they really are.

Only then, will they experience

## **The Earth Angel Awakening**

*The Other Side (book 3)*

There is an Angel who holds the world in her hands.
She is the **Angel of Destiny**.
Her actions will start the **ripples** that will **save humans**
from their certain demise.
In order for her to initiate the necessary changes, she
must travel to other **galaxies**, and call upon the most
**enlightened** and **evolved** beings of the Universe.
To save **humankind**.
When they agree, she wishes to prepare them for Earth
life, and so invites them to attend the Earth Angel Training
Academy, on
**The Other Side**


*The Twin Flame Reunion (book 4)*

The Earth Angels' missions are clear: **Awaken** the world,
and move humanity into the **Golden Age**.
But there is another reason many of the Earth Angels choose
to come to Earth.
To **reunite** with their **Twin Flames**.
The Twin Flame connection is deep, everlasting and intense,
and happens only at the **end of an age**. Many Flames
have not been together for millennia, some have never met.
Once on Earth, every Earth Angel longs to meet their Flame.
The one who will make them **feel at home**, who will
make living on this planet bearable.
But no one knows if they will actually get to experience
**The Twin Flame Reunion**

*The Twin Flame Retreat (book 5)*

The question in the minds of many Earth Angels
on Earth right now is:

Where is my **Twin Flame?**

Though many Earth Angels are now meeting their Flames,
the circumstances around their reunion can have
**life-altering** consequences.

If meeting your Flame meant your life would never be the
same again, would you still want to find them?

When in need of **support** and answers,
Earth Angels attend
**The Twin Flame Retreat**


*The Twin Flame Resurrection (book 6)*

Twin Flames are **destined** to meet. And when they are
meant to be together, nothing can keep them apart.

Not even **death**.

When Earth Angels go home to the Fifth Dimension too
soon, they have the **choice** to come back.

To be with their **Twin Flame**.

The connection can be so overwhelming, that some Earth
Angels try to resist it, try to push it away.

But it is **undeniable**.

When things don't go according to plan, the universe steps in,
and the Earth Angels experience
**The Twin Flame Ressurrection**

*The Twin Flame Reality (book 7)*
Being an Earth Angel on Earth can be difficult, especially
when it doesn't feel like home, and when there's a deep
longing for a realm or dimension where you feel you
**belong**.
Finding a Twin Flame, is like **coming home**.
Losing one, can be **devastating**.
Adrift, lonely, isolated... an Earth Angel would be forgiven
for preferring to go home, than to stay here
**without their Flame**.
But if they can find the **strength** to stay, to follow their
mission to **Awaken** the world, and fulfil their original
purpose, they will find they can be **happy** here.
Even despite the sadness of
**The Twin Flame Reality**

*The Twin Flame Rebellion (book 8)*
The Angels on the Other Side have a **duty** to **help** their
human charges, but **only** when they are **asked** for help.
They are not allowed to meddle with **Free Will**.
But a number of Angels are asked to break their
**Golden Rule**, and start influencing the human
lives of the Earth Angels.
Once the Angels start nudging, they find they can't stop, and
when the Earth Angels find out they are being manipulated
from the Other Side, they aren't happy.
Determined to **choose** their own **fate**,
the Earth Angels embark on
**The Twin Flame Rebellion**

*The Twin Flame Reignition (book 9)*
The **destiny** of many **Twin Flames** is changing.
Those destined to remain apart on Earth are hearing the
call to come **together.**

As things begin to shift and change, it suddenly it seems
**possible** for them to **reunite,** and have the lives they
always **dreamed** of.

But when **visions** and **dreams** of **Atlantis** begin to
plague the Earth Angels, and they try to work out their
meaning, what they **discover** may jeopardise
**The Twin Flame Reignition**

*The Twin Flame Resolution (book 10)*
When a Seer has a **vision** of the **Golden Age**, she takes
drastic action in order to make it happen.

The consequences of her actions are so **epic** that the lives
of every **Earth Angel** and every **human** on Earth will
be altered **forever.**

As well as the unions of all the
**Twin Flames.**

She enlists the help of two **Angels** to assist her in
**The Twin Flame Resolution**

# Visionary Collection:
## *Heaven dot com*

When Christina goes into hospital for the final time, and
knows that she is about to lose her battle with cancer, she
asks her boyfriend, James, to help her deliver messages to
her family and friends after she has gone.

She also asks him to do something for her, but she dies
before he can make it happen, and he finds it difficult to
forgive himself.

After her death, her messages are received by her loved
ones, and the impact her words have will change their lives
forever.

## *The Doorway to PAM*

Natalie is an ordinary girl who has lost her way. There
is nothing particularly special about her or her life. She
has no exceptional abilities. She hasn't achieved anything
miraculous. Her life has very little meaning to it.

Evelyn is the caretaker at Pam's. The alternate dimension
where souls at their lowest point find the answers they
need to turn their lives around. The dimension dreamers
visit, to help people while they sleep.

One ordinary girl, one extraordinary woman.
One fated meeting that will change lives.

## The Elphite

Ellie's life is just one long, bad case of déjà vu. She has lived her life before - a hundred times before - and she remembers each and every lifetime.
Each time, she has changed things, but has never managed to change the ending.
This time, in this life, she hopes that it will be different.
So she makes the biggest change of all - she tries to avoid meeting him.
Her soulmate. The love of her life.
Because maybe if they don't meet, she can finally change her destiny.
But fate has other ideas...

## I'm Here

When Marielle finds out that a guy she had a crush on in school has passed away, the strange occurrences of the previous week begin to make sense. She suspects that he is trying to give her a message from the other side, and so opens up to communicate with him, She has no idea that by doing so, she will be forming a bond so strong, that life as she knows it will forever be changed.

Nathan assumed that when he died, he would move on, and continue his spiritual journey. But instead he finds himself drawn to a girl that he once knew. The more he watches her, and gets to know her, he realises that he was drawn to her for a reason, and that once he knows what that is, he will be able to change his destiny.

## The Onist

Valerie is just a typical sixteen year old girl, until the moment that her consciousness slips into the body of another woman and causes a car crash.

She thinks it was just a vivid daydream until she finds a news article confirming the death of a woman the night before.

When Valerie begins to shift into the minds of other women, she finds herself in a dangerous situation, and must find a way to stop it before she becomes lost.

## Duelling Poets

For 30 days in 2012, Michelle and Victor wrote a poem a day, taking turns to choose the titles.

Michelle is an author, who was in her late 20s at the time, and Victor a retired journalist in his 70s. Their differing experiences and perspectives created contrasting poems, despite being written about the same topic.

In Duelling Poets, we invite you to read the poems and choose your favourites, then at the end, you can see which poet wins the duel for you.

# designs from a
# different planet

madappledesigns
.co.uk

# Earth Angel

# Sanctuary

Founded by Sarah Rebecca Vine in 2014, the Earth Angel Sanctuary has over 200 videos and audios (and growing), live calls every month and a Facebook family of like-minded souls.

With libraries including How-To Tutorials, an Energy and Vow Clearing Library, Rituals, Meditations, Activations and Bonuses, the Earth Angel Sanctuary has everything for those who have just discovered they are an earth angel to those who have been on their journey for a while and would love the additional love, support and growth it offers.

To find out more or join simply visit:

## earthangelsanctuary.com

(Monthly or yearly membership available)

"I believe that we will achieve peace on Earth and experience the Golden Age. My role is to awaken, inspire and support all light workers and earth angels to assist them in stepping into their power to help raise the vibration of our beautiful planet. I do that by sharing all the information I've learnt along my journey and I continue to do so..."

*Sarah Rebecca Vine - aka Starlight*

♥

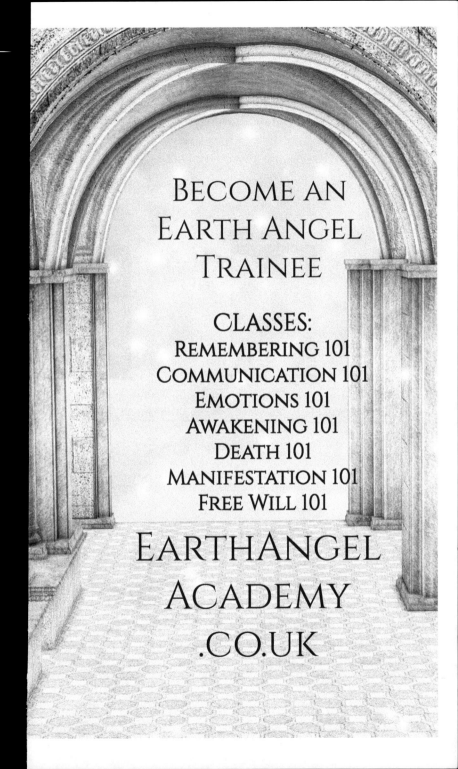

This book was published
by The Amethyst Angel.

A selection of books bought to publication by The Amethyst Angel.
To view more of our published books visit **theamethystangel.com**

We have a selection of publishing packages available or we can tailor a
package to suit each author's individual needs and budget. We also run
workshops for groups and individuals on 'How to publish' your own books.

For more information
on Independent publishing
packages and workshops offered
by The Amethyst Angel, please
visit **theamethystangel.com**

Lightning Source UK Ltd.
Milton Keynes UK
UKHW020637240820
368730UK00004B/117